Cynthia's Dreams

by

Art Myers

ISBN 978-1-7357208-6-9

Cover design by Janet L Blankenship

Contact Art Myers: artmyersbooks@gmail.com

Leokadiya Kashperova, her music, and Graham Griffiths
who found it for us.

Other Books by Art Myers

MY STORY
How A Young Boy From California
Ended Up An Old Man In Florida

ANDREW'S PIANO

ED ADAM CHASES A DREAM

A NEW LIFE FOR ROBERT JOHNSON

10,000 YEARS - Before Present

ED ADAMS TOUCHES THE STARS

Cynthia's Dreams

Preface

This book is being written as a sequel to my novel *Ed Adams Touches The Stars*. I do this because as I finished it I realized I had not answered a question that requires an answer. Cynthia believed that she had spent time with Sergei Rachmaninoff, helping with the composition of the first movement of his Concerto Number 2 and writing two compositions of her own. Not in dreams, but actually being there. She fell in love with him and he with her. This was, of course, impossible but finding the never before heard compositions that she knew, could flawlessly play and which had the notation of *1899 Cynthia* as their titles made her claims seem believable.

John, who with five scientist friends had developed the technology to travel back in time, wanted to find out exactly what had happened to make Cynthia believe as she did and why she was so sure she had experienced it. He promised Allison that was what he was going to do as *Ed Adams Touches The Stars* ends.

I will tell this story of what he finds in Cynthia's Dreams, but first I must provide you with a little more background about the characters that make it up.

In 2015 John's group had advanced their technology to the point they were ready to send someone back in time. They found an ideal candidate, one that felt he had nothing to lose and was willing to go back in time, Robert Johnson. He visited with Abraham Lincoln, Leonardo da

Vinci and, most importantly, Sergei Rachmaninoff. Some problems with the effects of the travel on the traveler had them improve their technique. Five years later, in 2020, they were able to have John join Robert and his partner, Sandra Williams, on their sailboat sending them back ten thousand years to visit the earliest native Americans then living in the Santa Cruz Mountains of California.

About this time Cynthia had a mental breakdown during her junior year at Interlochen College of Creative Arts. She was found asleep on a bench in the West Hollywood Greyhound Bus Station, not knowing who she was, having no money or identification and confused as to how she had gotten there. The responding police officers were only able to determine that she had come to visit Sergei Rachmaninoff, who had lived in his last home in nearby Beverly Hills until his death in 1943.

She was helped in her recovery by a friend of one of the police officers that led to her being employed as a caregiver for an elderly lady, Wilma Herman. Wilma had a grand piano in her small living room that had been given to her father by the Rachmaninoff family after his death. He had been his auto mechanic, helped around the house and could speak Russian and they had quickly become good friends. It is on this piano that Cynthia's talent as a pianist was to resurface.

The connections were made with these separate people when Ed Adams was the pianist for the Los Angeles Philharmonic's 2022 opener, presenting Sergei Rachmaninoff's Concertos Numbers 2 and 3. Robert Johnson and Sandra Williams were in attendance, hoping to meet and interest Ed in Robert's visit with Rachmaninoff. John's attendance was by chance having been given a donor's pass by one of his partners for this performance. But it is at the post concert donor's party that John, suspecting the reason for Robert's attempt to talk with Ed, watched as he and Sandra approached Ed and his wife, Julia, as they were talking with Wilma. All of them heard her say, "He was such a nice man. I knew him you know."

John's group had lost their long term lease at Stanford's SLAC facility as they now needed the abandoned space back for a new project. For John's group there was no way they could move the enormous amounts of equipment they had assembled for their back in time experiments. They did have time to make one more trip and John now had the one he wanted. Send Cynthia and Ed back to visit Rachmaninoff at what was to be his last Sunday open house on March 14, 1943, two weeks prior to his death on March 28th. Allison would lead and make the introductions to Natalia Rachmaninoff. At her suggestion Ed and Cynthia were seated at the two grand piano's in the lavishly decorated living room.

It was John's reasoning that Rachmaninoff must have done some composing during, and in between, his twenty-five seasons of concert touring. John believed he must have some works hidden away but very little was known of, or had been discovered, from after his immigration to America in 1918.

The story, Cynthia's Dreams, is introduced in the first chapter as this visit is in progress. It is in one of the boxes given to Cynthia by Rachmaninoff that contains the two compositions mentioned above. The story that follows provides John the answer to his question concerning Cynthia's dreams.

Chapter 1
Back in Time

As Ed finished the third movement's cadenza Cynthia, with perfect timing, started the second movement. It was only after the first few bars were played that Natalia realized something special was happening and that all her quests had stopped their conversations to listen.

Upstairs, in the bedroom at the top of the stairs, Sergei Rachmaninoff lay in his bed awake. The pain was getting worse. He ached all over, especially on his left side. His breathing was difficult and the ever present headache seemed to be worse than ever but he could hear the music clearly. His first thought was that his good friend Vladimir Horowitz was downstairs entertaining his guests. He knew almost immediately it wasn't him, however, but whoever it was playing was a good pianist. He listened carefully. He liked how the third movement was being played and when it finished another pianist started with the second movement on the second piano. He knew immediately that it was a woman playing and that she was good, every bit as good as the man.

Rachmaninoff struggled getting out of his bed. He wanted to go downstairs and meet these people. He had changed into his daytime clothes of slacks, collared shirt and light sweater that morning but was so weak and in such pain that he had just laid back down on his bed. He wished he hadn't wakened and would have passed away in his sleep, but now he wanted meet these pianists that were playing his compositions. His clothes were wrinkled and a quick glance in the bathroom mirror showed an old man near death. Dark circles under his eyes, his skin pale, blotched and covered with small bumps. His thoughts were why could he not die and get it over with. Paganini Variation 18 floated up to him and he had to stop thinking. He made what was the start of a smile and knew he had to make it downstairs.

A quick wash of his face and brushing what little hair he had left he shuffled out of his room. Hanging onto the railing he took one careful step after another until he made it to the foyer. Looking into the living room he could just see Cindy as she was playing the last part of Variation 18 and in Rachmaninoff's blurred vision she was the most beautiful woman he had ever seen. She turned his way and smiled. Not looking away she started playing the piece she had composed with him in her dreams. He winced as he listened and made his way to the piano. Sitting on the end of the bench, facing a way from the keyboard, he continued listening and said nothing.

Ed could see this happening and moved slightly to achieve a better view. Cindy was almost finished with her first piece and Rachmaninoff was sitting absolutely still. His emaciated back bent forward in an awkward position but his concentration intense. Cindy started the second piece. The one she had written herself and had also played for him in her dreams.

Rachmaninoff slowly moved, turning towards her, and speaking in an strained and hoarse voice said, "I know you from a long time ago. You played that for me. For me alone. I was young, healthy and working on my concerto number two. In Russia. You played me both of those pieces and I told you how good they were. I was engaged to Natalia but in those few minutes I fell in love with you. How can this be happening now. I am dying. Old. Almost helpless and you are as beautiful as I remember you."

A tear ran down his cheek but he didn't try to wipe it away. Cindy had finished as he told of his love and she reached over and wiped his tear away. "I knew it wasn't a dream. It happened and I want you to know I was in love with you then. I have your music now and that is enough for me. Know that."

Ed had started to play the first movement but started it as the first theme was developed. Rachmaninoff tried to stand up, staggered but caught himself. "I have some things you must have. You and your partner must have them. Come with me. They are in the library closet." He took Cindy's hand and they walked over to get Ed. He had no idea what was being said as Rachmaninoff and Cindy were both speaking in Russian but he understood by their gestures he was to go with them.

Three boxes were given to Cindy by Rachmaninoff with her promising she would see that his saved works would be brought to the public, both those finished and those needing further work. At Ed's suggestion they were taken by Wilma's father to their house to be stored there for Cindy and Ed to pick up later. This seemed satisfactory to Rachmaninoff and the last thing Ed saw of the boxes was Wilma's father exiting through the kitchen door outside carrying them to where they would stay for almost eighty years.

The trip had taken place from John's laboratory in Palo Alto on April 15, 2022 at 4:00 pm. The arrival point was a chosen location on the front lawn of the Beverly Hills home of Rachmaninoff at exactly 11:48 am, Sunday March 14, 1943 and lasted for 52.37 minutes. It was two days later at Wilma's small house that the boxes were retrieved, opened and the treasurers inside were first seen. Three concertos for piano, and even more valuable the concertos for each in orchestrated scoring. In between these two bundles of sheet music were six pages that should not have been there. Two melodies very familiar to the team that Cindy had played for them many times and that had triggered Rachmaninoff"s response leading to them being found. On the top of the first page of each was written, *1899 Cynthia.*

Chapter 2
2022

Rachmaninoff Concerto Number 7 was performed by the Desert Symphony Orchestra in Palm Desert, California, conducted by Ed Adams and featuring Cynthia Ashbaugh as the pianist, on Thursday, June 16, 2022 in the McCallum Theater. The rumors of the discovery of lost Rachmaninoff concertos had raced through the classical music world with lighting speed and by demand a matinee and evening repeat concert had been added for the following Saturday.

Sunday morning found the group at Ben and Jennifer's house for a late breakfast taken poolside. It had become such a common occurrence for the team it seemed only natural that the entire group would be there this morning.

John had purchased the house next door to Ben's when it was decided that the whole team would work together to take their findings public. Ed and Julia had bought the house on the other side years earlier when their twins arrived and the two houses had been connected by a enclosed passageway. Robert and Sandra took a room in John's house, Wilma was temporarily housed with Ben and Jennifer and Cindy and BJ, Ed and Julia's son, were now at home together in his old room in their house.

That morning John announced that he and Allison would be leaving for a ten day trip to Europe next Sunday and would have a meeting with the Serge Rachmaninoff Foundation representatives at Senar, on Lake Lucerne, in Switzerland. They had expressed interest in curating the original music sheets as had the Library of Congress. No decisions would be made but it would be a fun trip and John's first trip to Europe. Almost a honeymoon for he and Allison was the thinking of the rest of the group.

After all had finished breakfast John summarized their success and mentioned the trip to Europe. He had more on his mind as he had another interesting challenge to test his skills. He was unsure how to approach Cindy about this but he had told Allison about it the night before.

"There is no way Cindy could have been there with Rachmaninoff. No way possible. But there has to be an explanation of what we have absolute proof of what could not have happened, happened. I am going to find out how it did."

"You shouldn't go there. Not now, maybe not ever. Cindy's life has just begun again. You can't jeopardize that in any way!" was Allison's adamant response.

John had lain awake until he heard Allison's even breathing and then slipped out of bed. Before he left the room he looked at her sleeping soundly in his bed. How this could have happened this late in their lives was all part of the magic that had been his life the last few years. His team of Stanford drop outs had set up a venture capital firm that had become legend in the early Silicon Valley days and made them the riches needed to pursue the travel back in time development. Their first experiment, after he had made the the first travel tests, was Robert Johnson making trips to visit Abraham Lincoln, Leonardo da Vinci and Sergei Rachmaninoff.

Those trips had made it possible to set-up the Visiting History television programs that were successful and insured a financial reward for Robert and Sandra. John had them join him for his next trip back in time, on their sailboat, to visit the San Francisco Peninsula 10,000 years before the present. It was his, and his secretive group of five scientist's, crowning achievement until the visiting Rachmaninoff project fell into his lap.

It was the relationship of Cindy to Rachmaninoff that now was dominating his thoughts. It could not have happened but the proof seemed to be there that it had. He thought he had an answer but he had to be very careful as he was dealing with the life of a very important and loved person in all of their lives.

He went to his small office and opened his cell phone. scrolling down the contact list he touched Mike and pressed the call icon. Two rings later he was greeted with, "Hi John! What can I do for you?"

"Mike, the usual. A little research. Cynthia Anne Ashbaugh. This time her ancestry. I need to go back four or five generations. But first find out where her mother, father and brother are. This needs to be handled very discretely. Nothing is to get back to her just yet, if at all. That is very important." John paused for a moment and Mike waited as he knew another ask was coming.

"Another item is the Steinway Model C piano that was her grandmother's, or maybe great-grandmother's, that was brought over from Russia around 1912. It would be a Hamburg build, late 1800s to no later than 1912. Where is it and can I get hold of it?"

"Always a great adventure, John. A pleasure to go hunting for you. I will send you what I have by Wednesday," and the connection was broken.

John smiled. He had worked together with Mike since the venture capital days. As a researcher and detective he had no peer. He knew he would have most of the information he needed to start his search on Wednesday and it would be enough to know if he should continue. He would go no further than this if Cindy did not want to go there. He wanted her to encourage him to try to find the answers as to how what could not have happened, happened.

A smile formed on John's face and became even broader as he slipped back into bed next to Allison. She moved slightly toward him and gently touched his arm, not wakening. He felt that his life could not get any better than it was at this moment and minutes later he also was asleep.

Chapter 3
2022

As breakfast was finished and the cleanup done the group began to gather in the music room. It was Ben's former living room, adjacent to and open to the kitchen and dining area. In the far corner was Ed's mother's 1925 Steinway parlor grand piano which one of Ben's oldest friends had located, had restored and given to Ed at a time when it was needed.

Before John and Allison made their way back inside, he had been trying to make discrete observations of his latest interest, Cynthia Ashbaugh. She was dressed in simple clothes of T-shirt, shorts and sandals. The evening before in her full length concert gown had shown the exceptionally beautiful woman she was and this morning she seemed to be an even more beautiful young girl. She and BJ were having the conversations new lovers have, totally lost in their own world.

Allison poked John in the ribs and told him to stop looking at Cindy and to join her in the music room. Ed had placed some music sheets on the music rack and was starting to play a bit of what was on them. When Cindy heard this she took BJ's hands, pulled him up, kissed him soundly, and said, "Your father is calling me to join him. He is playing something new and it is meant for four hands to play. Come along and let us entertain you."

Cindy went straight to the piano and sat down on

Ed's right and looked carefully at the sheet music. He had opened the Rachmaninoff"s Six Pieces To Valse scoring, Cindy looked it over quickly and remembered she had played it before. A quick nod to Ed and they played, sight reading, to the end.

Ed found it not quite right for the room and turning to Cindy suggested they play their game of playing Concerto Number 2 in a way they had created during some of their practice sessions when it had become tiresome. He started and, without slowing down, moved to let Cindy slide into position and continue without so much as a break. Making room for the other was the signal and the exchange had to be made quickly. The game was to catch the other not ready to continue.

It was fun for them and a treat for the rest as they caught on to what was being done. The partnership Ed and Cindy had made with each other could not be ignored. It was special but in no way indicated anything but professionals exhibiting their skills. The recital was finished with Cindy playing the second movement solo and it was played as it should be played.

It was time for the team to while away the remainder of the day. BJ suggested to Cindy a walk along El Paseo and share an ice cream cone. Smiles were exchanged and they made their exit.

John and Allison headed toward their house and he was already planning his strategy for engaging Cindy to the discovery about her past and her relationship to Rachmaninoff. Allison picked up on this and taking his hand lead him to their bedroom. "I am going to give you, my young lover, a test on your ability to do two things at the same time."

She started laughing, telling him she was only kidding but John answered her in a different way. He wasn't going to have the information he really needed until Wednesday and so why waste such a perfectly good Sunday afternoon. It wasn't wasted and John could indeed do two things at the same time. The latter he would keep to himself and it was possible that it helped him with the other.

Cindy and BJ walked along El Paseo window shopping until they got to the ice cream parlor. A double scoop, mocha chocolate chip atop butter pecan, on a sugar cone was ordered. They found a small table in the breeze way that had a seating area and which they had to themselves. Passing the cone back and forth they had almost finished the cone when Cindy started the conversation.

"John kept looking at me this morning. They were just glances, maybe held just a moment too long. Only appreciative, I think. Nothing more."

"I saw it, too," BJ commented and then continued, "You are so good to look at. You probably haven't noticed but I occasionally take a long look at you. Not always just in appreciation, however."

He then started a more serious conversation on how he was certain John now had a new project and that it would involve them both. She was the subject and he would be her support. "Do you want me to tell you what I think it is about?" BJ asked, afraid of what it was he was thinking of telling her. That John would be wanting to know the answer to what her dreams meant. That she couldn't have actually been there at that time.

Cindy surprised BJ by quickly answering, "He

wants to discover how my dreams of being with Rach-maninoff have been proven by the music found in one of the boxes that I know how to play and Sergei recognizing me on our visit."

She then surprised him even more, "I am not afraid to go there. In fact I think I should, and find out what happened. I will need you to be with me. With me through what ever I have to go through. You have to be there with me!"

Chapter 4
2022

Monday came and went. Ed and Cindy had already decided that Concerto Number 5 should be next. This had been agreed upon by the Desert Symphony Orchestra director and the word had already gotten out. An early September date was being set and the request for seats were being received. They would follow the first format of a Thursday night premier followed by a Saturday matinee and an evening concert.

Ed and Cindy were beginning the memorization and playing complete parts as they did so. They had no doubt that Rachmaninoff had composed another quality concerto and that it might even rival Number 7. BJ and Julia were busy preparing the scores for the orchestra and the print shop was busy. John had, of course, already ordered all the supplies necessary and production was going smoothly.

Robert and Sandra had headed back up to Point Reyes Station to take care of a few things at their small house and on their sailboat. They were well under way in writing their novel. All the receipts, notes and scraps in the third box were now starting to make some sense and an outline was forming. The dates, places and timing were leading them on to a life that had many possibilities to have been much more intriguing than what the current literature offered. Especially in his personal life as was tracked by the receipts which indicated events that had not been covered in his biographies. Many seemed to be at the same time he met new acquaintances, especially women.

Ben, Jennifer and Wilma were watching it all and contributing now and then when they saw something they could offer of value. Wilma was beginning to realize she had a place to call home with those who wanted her to be there. She wasn't ready to leave her place in Beverly Hills yet, but the idea of doing so was no longer frightening.

On Wednesday at 10:00 am a file was in John's email and was soon downloaded and printed out. Ten double spaced pages, a number of which were a single paragraph and a few only a single sentence.

He retired to his small office and laid the report on top of his empty desk. Allison had followed him in and sat in the largest of the two chairs. They exchange looks and smiles formed on each of their faces. "We have a project," was John's announcement. "Yes we do," was Allison's response. She had several of the popular biographical books on Rachmaninoff, including Sergei Rachmaninoff, A Lifetime In Music, Rachmaninoff's Cape, Critical Lives Sergei Rachmaninoff and a number of printouts from internet searches on her lap and began to lay them out on John's desk top that was to closest to her.

"You know what we are looking for don't you?" John asked, and already knowing what the answer would be continued, "Cindy could not have been there in person. That is impossible. She was there in her mind. Having the evidence we have it had to be learned from someone near her. A great-grandmother who had been there and told her little great-granddaughter the stories of the most exciting things that had happened in her life as a young woman.

She must have been Russian, a talented pianist, composer, near Rachmaninoff's age, attractive to him and willing to be his lover. The period is somewhere around 1899 to 1901. We can deduce from what we have on the music sheets and which Cindy knows how to play must have been taught to her. Or there are some scores, or at least were, that Cindy could have learned from. We also can deduce that whoever it was had to look a little bit like our Cynthia."

Allison held John's gaze as he spoke and could not repress her smile. "John, you make my life so exciting. I can't ever remember being so ready to start something like this. I can visualize the events that took place. The old woman holding little Cynthia in her lap while telling the stories of her romance with the handsome, young Rachmaninoff. Her helping him through this most difficult time in his life. Then teaching her young prodigy how to play those special pieces she composed." She paused for a moment and John let her take her time. "So far I have read nothing that indicates that happened but there are many clues that make it clear that it must have happened that way. I am totally ready for this, John! I can hardly wait to get started." She held up her printed up papers and laid her hand on the books as she smiled at him with a look he now cherished.

Chapter 5
1899-1900

Sergei Rachmaninoff had taken only a few steps after closing the big outer doors of the apartment building into the early morning cold and snow and his mood had quickly dropped to match it. It had been snowing off and on for a week in Moscow and the sidewalks had about four inches of fresh snow on top of a glaze of ice. He had dressed in his warmest clothes and was wearing his best winter shoes but was already feeling the chill which was also reaching into his heart.

He had purchased his ticket for the 8:15 am train to Saint Petersburg to visit his mother. She was still living in the same apartment his family had moved into when the last of their estates had been foreclosed on by his father's creditors. She was now living there alone. He wasn't look-ing forward to spending the Christmas holiday there but felt the obligation as none of his remaining siblings could, or wanted to, be there with her.

Sergei's good friend Fyodor Chaliapin had given him the keys to his apartment in Saint Petersburg for his two to three week stay and that would provide for some much needed time alone to make the visit tolerable. He was hoping to use the time to accomplish some compos-ing and the apartment had a fine piano and writing desk which would suit his needs.

He had entered a period of almost total collapse

since the debut of his first symphony, nearly three years ago, was so poorly received. He had gone into a period of self doubt, depression and thinking he might never be able to compose anything of merit again. Only his virtuosity as a pianist and skill as a conductor had given any meaning to his life since he had graduated from the Conservatory. He was now, as a Free Artist, having to support himself for the first time and it wasn't going that well.

His one act opera Aleko had won the gold medal from the school and he had been presented by his instructor with a gold watch as he graduated. He had completed his first symphony and it was to be his debut as a composer. He hadn't listened to advice about a few changes to the score and unfortunately the orchestra did not prepare well. Glazunov, the conductor for it's debut, did not help either. Some even thought him to be drunk at the podium. March 15, 1897 was his personal disaster and he was still trying to recover some confidence after it's debacle.

The Satin family, especially his mother's sister and her two daughters, Natalia and Sophie, were his angels. Not only did they provide moral support but also financial help, a home and adopted him into their family.

None of this was being thought about as Sergei trudged carefully through the snow that covered the slippery cobblestone sidewalks. What had happened as he said his goodbyes to Natalia in the lobby of the apartment was on his mind. He was becoming more aware of her in a less sisterly manner as the years had passed. She had wanted more than that ever since she had first met him and had watched silently as he mooned over his teenage crush for Vera Skalon, the youngest of the three Skalon girls whose family shared the summer estate of the Satin's.

When Vera's mother found about the seventeen year old Sergei's fondness for her fifteen year old daughter she put a stop to it. At least as for them during the summers. Distance apart took care of the rest of the year and for the last two summers Vera's health had her mother taking her to another location for a better climate. Sergei wrote to her for two more years using the older sisters as the go between as he had been forbidden to write to her directly.

Ten years had passed and another intense infatuation with the wife of one of the members of the orchestra he was conducting, Anna Aleksandrovna, could also not be ignored by Natalia. But this morning, as the forlorn Rachmaninoff was standing in the foyer in his heavy overcoat holding his small suitcase, she pulled his head down and kissed him. "I love you Sergei Rachmaninoff, I have always loved you. Don't break my heart again. Come home to me here and let me love you. Love me." She turned away and quickly headed down the hall to the elevator and was gone before he could think of what to say.

It was this he was thinking of as he continued walking. He arrived at the station not remembering the walk and thinking that he had much more to think about than just himself and he must make the effort to do that. Maybe loving someone who loved you would be better than what he had experienced so far in his life.

With ticket in hand he entered the first economy carriage and his day seemed to disintegrate even more. His train travel had always been at least a class above this and the sight of the two rows of double bench seats, separated by a middle isle and already half filled by a scruffy lot, sent him into almost total despair. Twelve hours seated in this manner was not what he was used to but he had so little money he couldn't afford anything better.

He found an empty bench and took the window seat. Minutes later he had a very fat male seatmate that smelled of alcohol and garlic. It seemed a dark cloud had descended over his being. Closing his eyes he wasn't sure he would ever want to open them again.

Chapter 6
1899-1900

The train had reached full speed, at least for the conditions in Moscow at that time, and the rhythm of the steels wheels on the track had evened out. It was of no help to Sergei, with his eyes still closed he could hear his seatmate opening a paper bag and the odor of some type of spiced sausage sandwich reached his nostrils.

"Sergei, Sergei Rachmaninoff, could I have a word with you?" was asked in perfect Russian with an American accent.

Almost afraid to open his eyes he squinted at it's source. As the man came into focus Sergei could see the person addressing him was tall, well dressed, handsome and sporting a friendly smile. He mumbled out a rather feeble, "Yes, Sir."

"Why don't you get your suitcase and overcoat and come with me. It will be worth your while, I assure you." It was said with such sincerity that Sergei immediately stood, got his suitcase and coat and was almost desperately trying to get passed his seatmate to the aisle. The fat man grunted something unintelligible and grasped his paper bag against his chest, crushing whatever it's contents was, but didn't offer to move.

Sergei made it to the isle with an apology to the fat man and was quickly following the gentleman that was saving him from drowning in his own despair.

They quickly walked forward through the three economy carriages until they reached the first of the first class ones. The gentleman turned around and offered his hand which Sergei took in a welcomed handshake.

"My name is Samuel Beckman. I am an American businessman here in Russia, now for three years, with my family. My wife, Rose, and my daughter, Cynthia. We have a compartment and would like to invite you to make the rest of the trip to Saint Petersburg as our guest. We have one other guest with us you may know, or know of, Leokadiya Kashperova."

"Kashperova. Oh yes! She is quite a coming star, both as a pianist and a composer," Sergei saying this fast as his excitement of this good fortune was overcoming all his dread and he actually made a smile that lit up his face. Samuel didn't realize it at the time but he had just witnessed something that for years to come he would mention to others about his first meeting with the man that would become a world famous musician, but who very seldom smiled.

Samuel continued telling Sergei that they had attended the concert the night before at the Large Hall of the Nobility and enjoyed his performance. It was his daughter that saw him enter the economy car and who had insisted that he come and rescue him from such a fate, regardless of why it had happened.

They had reached the door to the compartment and Samuel knocked, the door opened and Sergei Rachmaninoff's life was to make one of the most important change of directions that it was to ever have. The young and beautiful face of Cynthia Beckman smiled her welcome and said in an clear and melodic voice, "I told you it was him!

I was sure of it! Welcome into our lives Sergei Vasil'evich Rachmaninoff." She offered her hand and it was taken by Sergei in disbelief that any thing like this could possibly be happening.

Chapter 7
2022

John picked up the report from Mike and looked over the first page. It had only the title centered at the top, Cynthia, and at the bottom of the page,1/10. He smiled at that and thought Mike was a man of few words, but each word had meaning when he described what was important.

The next two pages were a summary of what was already known about Cindy from the time she had arrived at the bus depot in West Hollywood and found her way to being Wilma Herman's caregiver.

He looked up and saw Allison was intently reading one of the pages she had down loaded from the internet. He thought how pretty she was, even at seventy-five. To him she looked much younger. That she was here, with him, seemed a miracle. His only friend of any merit during his childhood and when he was seven, and she fourteen, her family had moved away and took her with them.

He continued watching her and thought back over those sixty years. He had never made another friendship like that again until these last few years. His business partners were friends but for what ever reasons they were never really close friends in a personal way. He had met many women over those years but few he thought he could ever love, or even really like. Those he did find of interest always seemed to be happily married, or were lesbians. He realized he now had someone he could love and who seemed to be loving him. He lifted up the report to mask his face as a few tears had begun to slide down his cheeks.

Page four of ten was headed simply piano, in capital letters. Photo copied below was a receipt for settlement of storage fees on a legal foreclosure document citing six month overdue rental and legal fees. The new lessor of the unit, and owner of it's contents, was made out in John's name and a paid in full receipt by a Chase Bank card for $18,742.87 covering the unpaid rental amount, legal fees and payment for the seized contents, including the piano. A new lock was to be placed on the unit and both keys forwarded to the new lessee in Palm Desert, California. John's laughter roused Allison from her concentration on what she was reading. "What's so funny, my funny little man?" was said in an affectionate way along with a bright smile that John was getting used to seeing and treasured.

"We now own another piano. I am sure it is an early Steinway Model C that has come to us from Russia just before the revolution of 1917. It resides in a Wauseon, Ohio storage unit and I think I will be getting a phone call from Mike tomorrow morning. He will tell me what else he found. We have a place to start. Not an answer but a place to start looking for it. Steinway places a serial number on every piano they build and I am certain we will be able to find out who was the original purchaser of this one, the date of purchase and location of the delivery.

"The legal document lists Alan Ashbaugh as the renter, dated as rented on February 15, 2019 with twenty-four months paid in advance. Page five will tell me much of what happened in our Cindy's family during the time the piano has been in that storage room." John moving page five into position as he said this.

Glancing down over the page he then looked to-ward Allison and speaking softly said, "We will have to keep this to ourselves for the time being. It is a very sad story about a good family's tragedy."

Cindy's father,"Ash", had been born in Wauseon, Ohio. He had gone through high school there with good grades and numerous athletic awards. He chose not to go to college and took a job in the local metals foundry where his father was a foreman. Three years later a very attrac-tive young woman, just graduated from the University of Wisconsin, arrived as the new high school music teacher. She was from Appleton, Wisconsin and about the same age as Ash, one Shirley Catherine Mason. A year later they married and in another year their first child was born, a boy, naming him Andrew, followed two years later by a daughter, Cynthia, and after three years more by a second daughter, Jacqueline.

The sudden death of Shirley's father a few days af-ter Cindy was born had her mother, and her mother's mother, join the growing family. Ash had a small addition added to the house which consisted of a large room for the two ladies with twin beds, living area, bathroom with a walk-in shower and a kitchenette. It was a nice place for them and they became full time sitters for the children in their early years. Grandma Beth and great-grandmother Anne.

The grandmothers house was decorated with much of their furniture and also housed the Steinway Parlor Grand that had made it's way from Russia when great-grandmother Anne and her husband had fled Russia as the revolution stirred. (This was found to not be the case, but had been assumed so for years.)

Ash had wanted a change from the job at the foundry position as he didn't see his future there. So he, with some financial help from his father, all of his savings and the promise of a steady salary from Shirley's teaching position had the young newly weds buying a local pizza parlor. The learning curve was steep but with hard work and being well known by most of the people in Wauseon, their business was successful.

Things went very good for the new family. The restaurant was profitable. Shirley was liked at the school, enjoyed her teaching position and made her name as a pianist. It was around Cynthia's fourth birthday that the first indications of her possibly being a prodigy began to surface. With minimal help from her mother, and grandmothers, she started skillfully playing short scores she heard on the radio or TV. As Shirley became aware of this talent she could see a future for her little girl that she had once dreamed of for herself but did not quite have the talent, or drive, to accomplish.

It had started with Cindy spending her early childhood with her grandmothers playing the piano and sitting in her great-grandmother Anne's lap hearing the stories about her mother, a talented pianist, who had met Sergei Rachmaninoff in Russia, having been in love with him, and he with her. Stories lovingly told, over and over again, to the small child as she was rocked to sleep.

By the time Cindy was six there was no doubt of her talent. She was playing much beyond her age and had a memory that amazed everyone. As Shirley's concentration on her daughter began to intrude on her care of the rest of the family, the problems began to mount.

At about this time Ash had decided to buy the franchised pizza restaurant out by the I-80 freeway exit into town. He quickly realized it required much more management acumen than had been needed for the local one, the stress on him had increased and his time spent with his family was drastically reduced.

It was then that a cascade of events occurred that had the family disintegrate in a matter of ten years.

Chapter 8
2022

John was compiling much of this in his mind from the main points made in Mike's report. He realized many years before that he had this special gift for imagination. Finding a simple arrowhead in Big Basin Park in northern California had him taking great imagined adventures with the native Indians, roaming about the park as he talked with them as if they were there. Talking about hunting and gathering, life and death, the forest and wildlife, all in great detail. He had spent hours and hours an only child in an adult world. Maybe he still was, was his thinking as he picked up the report to continue

He looked up and saw that Allison was not there and another smile crossed his face. She was beginning to know him so well that when he had gone silent and was in deep concentration that she should leave him alone and come back later to talk. It was becoming a very good relationship and he was welcoming it.

He was certain of what was coming next and knew it wasn't going to be pleasant. The recession of 2008 was looming and things were not going to be good for the small family in Wauseon.

About mid 2008 Ash decided he would never make the pizza parlor near the Interstate profitable and sold it at a substantial loss. Ten year old Cynthia's progress on the piano was such that Shirley was spending almost all of her free time with her and she had already played in a number of competitions. These were very simple programs with more of a feel of recitals, each participant receiving an award. They were preparation for what was to come.

It was 2011 that the first real tragedy occurred. Jacqueline, ten years old, and just beginning to exhibit what a beautiful young lady she would become, fell ill. First it was thought to be the flu, then the fatigue, loss of appetite, and headaches suddenly got much worse. A specialist was visited in Toledo and she immediately summoned a second opinion from a leukemia specialist. The prognosis was dire. It had progressed so rapidly that there was no treatment that would warrant the short survival possible versus the pain the patient would suffer from it's administration. Two weeks later Jacqueline was put to rest in the small cemetery in Wauseon and with her was buried most of the happiness of the Ashbaugh family.

Andrew had taken it the hardest. He had become Jacqueline's closest family member. Ash's long hours running the restaurants had robbed her of a full time father figure and Shirley's concentration on Cynthia's development as a pianist had left her with the aging grandmothers and him. What was a surprise to all was that he had relished it. They had become much more than just brother and sister, true friends.

It was a relationship that was beneficial to both and her passing had left Andrew with little as a family member. Upon graduation from high school in 2014 he joined the Navy. It was a total surprise to the family as he had never discussed such plans, nor any of his plans for the future for that matter. There was more of course. As the recruiter went through the general paperwork which included questions on grades, interest, and preferences the fact that Andrew was passably fluent in the Russian language had him enrolled in the Naval Post Graduate School in Monterrey, California. A door was opened for the rather forlorn and undecided youth from Wauseon, Ohio and he walked through it.

Cynthia's life was also about to change in a dramatic way. Her younger sister's death was weighing on her as was the increasing pressure being placed on her by her mother to make a name for herself as a pianist. Jacqueline's death seemed to make her mother even more frantic for her to attain success. This was coupled with the fact that she was going through all the traumas of puberty, having her first periods and constantly being chased by the boys. Her transformation from a girl to a woman was such that her looks could not be missed. She was a beautiful young woman, poised beyond her age with a smile that could melt the heart of anyone who was presented it.

There was more as there always is. The competitions many times required selection from specific lists of composers and compositions. Cynthia was raised on Rachmaninoff, both his music and the tales of his relationship to the family. Handed down by her great-grandmother Anne was the stories of her mother's brief affair with the great artist but also the Russian language. Fortunately she could sight read musical scores and had that innate ability for memorization that all great pianist have. Shirley was beginning to realize her part in Cynthia's progress was no longer adequate to propel her further. The sole purpose of her life seemed to be ebbing away along with a reason to live.

Cynthia's Dreams

The Grandmothers took their turn in leaving this earth. First was Shirley's mother at age seventy-three in 2011 just four months after Jacqueline and then Anne at one hundred and four in the first week of 2012. Andrew would be leaving after his graduation in 2014 and Ash was having some problems with finding a meaning for his life. He would sell the pizza parlor that same year.

The decision was made to get Cynthia qualified for the 2012 Cleveland International Piano Competition for Young Artists in August of that year. The preliminaries commenced in March and Cynthia had to learn a number of new and difficult works by a variety of composers, none of which were Rachmaninoff. Never the less her success was astounding. Not only was her talent as a pianist excellent, her stage presence was unmatched. A beautiful, fourteen year old girl, with looks well beyond her age, matched her performance and easily had her make it into the final thirty-six for the competition and then into the final twenty-four.

She chose from the required list Beethoven:Sonata for Piano no 23 in F minor, Op.57 and Chopin:Etudes (12) for Piano, Op.25 and then added a not allowed two pieces of unknown work only identified at the last minute as *1899 Cynthia.*

She was disqualified but was voted first as for audience favorite much to the consternation of the judging panel. Needless to say she made the headlines of the next day's newspaper, The Plain Dealer.

With lighting speed Cindy was offered a full ride scholarship to Interlochen Arts Academy, located in northwest Michigan, with a promise of a like scholarship into the Interlochen College of Creative Arts upon graduation.

It was just 250 miles from home.

The scholarship was accepted and in the Fall of 2012 the Ashbaugh home was down to three and in less than two years more down to Shirley and Ash who had become strangers. In 2019 they decided on a separation, which was how they had been living ever since Andrew had left home.

Shirley continued her teaching music at the high school but was now just a teacher and not the guiding light she had once been. Ash had sold the pizza parlor and they sold the house buying a town home just a few blocks away. The few possessions they wanted to keep but didn't fit into the town home were placed in a storage unit. Included was the cherished parlor grand piano that had come to America from Russia over one hundred years ago.

Ash went to Alaska searching for a new life and on crab boat as a part time crew member was lost at sea. A violent storm had surprised the captain and cost the lives of two other crew members on another boat. 2020 was a bad year for the Alaskan crabbers.

Shirley died of an apparent fentanyl overdose soon after the news of Ash's accident had reached her. Since Ash had departed the only thing left for her had been watching Cindy's progress at Interlochen. Even that had started to wain as her life became more independent and their closeness had dissolved to almost indifference.

At the service two more headstones were added to the Ashbaugh plot and this time a crowd was there. One should never underestimate the relationships that a beloved school teacher has had on those that were their students.

Andrew could tell Cindy was having trouble with

all this and tried to comfort her as best he could. She had asked him to take care of things for her as far as the town home and their inheritance. That at some time in the future she would like to have the piano but there was nothing else she cared to keep. Maybe some of the photo albums would be nice to share with him. She signed a notary of republic and left the cemetery to drive back to Interlochen.

He watched her as she walked back to her car and felt sad to see his remarkable sister look so defeated. She had always been a winner. Her star had always shined and given him hope. He felt he should go after her and find out if he could help, but didn't. One month later he was on a military transport plane headed for a destination he would learn of when he got there. The United States Government needed someone who could speak and understand Russian in a top secret location. It would be five years before he came back and then it would be him that needed the help.

Chapter 9
1899-1900

The introductions were made quickly but Sergei Rachmaninoff was not paying his full attention and still hadn't released the handshake with Cynthia Beckman when they were repeated a second time. Her mother, Rose Beckman, and the other young woman, Leokadiya Kashperova, then made his acquaintance. Cynthia's laughter helped cover his embarrassment and her smile had Sergei at a loss for words.

Seating was likewise quickly arranged in the six passenger compartment by Samuel, with he and Rose seated on the forward seats and the girls seated on either side of Segrei on the facing bench. Compared to the economy section this was luxurious and on his left was the most beautiful young woman he had ever sat next to and on his right was one of the most talented pianists in Russia, who although somewhat plain in comparison, had her own beauty.

Sergei was trying to say something to start the conversation and it was obvious neither of the others planned to help him out. Looking down he realized his bony knees stuck up higher than the others and for a moment he had the illusion that they didn't belong to him. A box that was the size that held sheet music was on the table and he asked to whomever would answer what might be in it.

Leokadiya was first and said that they had brought a few things she and Cynthia were working on.

"I would certainly like to see what the best of the them all has been writing," was his reply to her, quoting the well known praise given by Anton Rubinstein of his prized student as she graduated from his premier class at the Saint Petersburg Conservatory.

This caused Cynthia to enthusiastically clap her hands together and gently elbow him in the side. An appreciated smile from Leokadiya lit up her face which Sergei was beginning think was more attractive than his first impression had been.

He had passed the first hurdle in a relationship with these new friends that would make the next two weeks most important for his future.

After a bit more casual conversation between the five the next question to Sergei was where he was staying in Saint Petersburg. He confided he was making the trip to visit his mother for Christmas but had been offered the apartment of his best friend, Fyodor Chaliapin, for his stay and that it was in the same building as Rimsky-Korsakov's. This brought on so much laughter from all four that he had to wait until it had died down to find out what had amused them. Samuel finally asked, "Who wants to tell him?"

"I do!" was Cynthia's almost shout and she continued, "Our apartment is on the second floor directly below Fyodor's and Leokadiya's is on the fifth floor above Korsakov's third floor apartment. We are all going to be together. What a fun time we will be having," was said in delight with another elbow poke in the smiling Sergei Rachmaninoff's ribs.

This had the ladies taking turns describing the active Tuesday evenings at Leokadiya's apartment and the Wednesday evenings with the Rimsky-Korsakov's. Mainly social, always entertaining and once in a while revealing how good at what they did so many of them were.

Sergei was beginning to think he had gone to heaven, tried to sit still and hide the emotions he was feeling. Could this be real. It was and the next thing he knew Leokadiya was handing him six sheets of scoring. The scoring was neatly written and he began reading it.

Like most gifted pianist and composers he could hear the music he was reading. He read the first sheet, then the second and third which on the last bar filled in had the double line indicating the end of that piece. He look about the room and could see all the eyes were on him. "That is beautiful. Wonderful music. I want to play it on a grand piano. Fyodor told me he has an upright but do you have a small grand, or really good upright. As I understand it Rimsky-Korsakov still doesn't have a piano in his apartment."

Again there was some polite laughter but this time a serious answer. Leokadiya had a small grand and Cynthia had one of the newest small Steinway parlor grand pianos which she loved. Even Korsakov had played it and was thinking it was time to have a piano and this is what he would choose to have. He had decided that his way of composing, and judging other's work, of just reading the scores and listening to what he saw with his eyes, that maybe it was time to listen to it with his ears.

Lunch had been ordered and Sergei thought he best leave his sausage, cheese and bread in the tightly secured package in his suitcase. As the pleasant odor of a quality soup drifted up from the large bowls he thought of his seatmate in economy unwrapping what ever he had stuffed in his greasy case. He said a silent prayer of thank you to any who might be listening.

The afternoon went along as pleasantly as had the morning. Samuel had some business papers out and was concentrating in a manner that had him tune out the others. Rose had a book she was reading and appeared very content with whatever it was. The three others had something else to look at as Rachmaninoff had removed a thick folder from his case which had written in rather sloppy script Concerto No 2 for Piano.

It contained well over a hundred sheets and he sorted down through the bundle until he reached the second movement. He changed places with Cynthia and handed her about forty sheets. The transcription was not nearly as neat as Cynthia's but still readable. She concentrated on the first page, then handed it to Leokadiya. The two of them read through to the end.

Leokadiya spoke first, whispering, "That is great. Truly great music, Sergei. Do you have the third and first movements done?" was asked in an reverent manner.

"I have the third done. It is as good as the second but the first movement has me beaten. I don't want to admit it but I think I have developed writer's block and need help. In fact I am to start having sessions with a Dr. Dahl on January ninth who will use hypnoses to help me get my confidence back and make it possible to compose again."

It had come out as confession. Leokadiya had already heard about his depression, and lack of composing, caused by the terrible reception of his first symphony on it's debuting after he had received his Free Artist award from the Moscow Conservatory.

Cynthia took a long look at Sergei and could read his thoughts, as his shoulder's had slumped and the unhappiness showed on his face. What a handsome man he was when he smiled and as she nodded towards Leokadiya told him, "We are going to fix that little problem on the First Movement and you are going to return to Moscow in two weeks the happiest man in Russia." She turned to Leokadiya and finished with, "Should be a good project for the two of us over the holidays, don't you think? Can you think of anything more fun than making this sad boy the happiest man in Russia?"

"Cynthia, let's get started right now! Let us see Number 2, First Movement," was directed to Sergei and he handed over about sixty sheets of scoring.

Chapter 10
1899-1900

Sergei Rachmaninoff didn't know what to do. The two girls were going through his scoring, sheet after sheet, occasionally stopping, making a comment on this or that, showing a smile or a frown. Several times in the first few sheets he would see Leokadiya smile and then she would hum the melody, or even sing a few notes. She had a beautiful soprano voice and he would recognize what she was reading.

Samuel broke into his concentration, suggesting they go get a coffee in the restaurant carriage which he gladly accepted. It was several carriages forward and the walk felt good. They stopped for a quick visit to the toilet and then found a private place to sit. It was obvious to Sergei that Cynthia's father was going to have a talk with him about his daughter.

"You have just met two extraordinary women. You know that and you know they both want you as a friend, maybe even more. Leokadiya is your age and Cynthia is twenty-two. I want you to consider only friendship for both the next few weeks. We, meaning myself, Rose and Cynthia will be returning to America leaving here on the last day of January, if not before. We will travel to Paris first for a week and then on to Amsterdam. Hopefully by the end of February we will be in our home in Cleveland, Ohio. I want Cynthia to be with us in the same condition that she is in now. I trust you understand what I mean by this!"

He was looking directly into Sergei's eyes as he said this and that look told Sergei all he needed to know. His indecision as to how to handle his rising desires for Cynthia had been decided for him. "Yes, Sir, I understand," was answered and, "Good!" was Samuel's single word response.

Next, Samuel described his work, what he was doing here in Russia and why Cynthia and Rose were here with him. Simply put, he sold farming equipment. More honestly put he looked for talent and inventions. And not just farming equipment but in all fields of industry. He was not a spy in any sense of the word, had no ties with any governments and didn't want any. He was a searcher for opportunities and was very good at what he did.

He also could speak and read seven languages and had been hired on a retainer to spend three years in Russia and visit several of the western countries nearby including Poland and Ukraine.

They had rented the Saint Petersburg apartment knowing that Rimsky-Korsakov lived there and also that Leokadiya Kashperova was there, as she would be Cynthia's piano teacher that had been arranged for in advance. It was hoped that opportunities for her to be in the presence of such people would help develop her talents as a pianist. Cynthia had studied both French and Russian in school and was now proficient in both.

It had worked out well for them but it was time for them to return home. He told Sergei he had been very successful over this period, was hoping it had helped Cynthia achieve her goals in music and that she could find happiness back home.

He left it a that, remarked what good coffee it was and they headed back to the compartment.

Rose had a similar conversation with Cynthia and Leokadiya and that she thought Sergei was a very nice young man but needed time to sort out some demons that seemed to be plaguing him at the moment.

"He will become our best friend and we will see to it that he is to leave it at that," was Cynthia's response but Leokadiya seemed less enthusiastic of the friendship idea. She did realize that as for now it would be Cynthia's problem but Sergei Rachmaninoff had a talent she would like to get closer to. It would be his music first, and it also would probably be that way in the future as well, was her thinking.

The train had made good time, even in the cold, winter conditions and pulled into the station a few minutes before seven o'clock. A horse drawn carriage was hired and they soon were standing in front of the apartment building on Zagorodny Prospekt. They entered and went to the Beckman's apartment and Rose offered to put together something for an evening snack and suggested Sergei find Fyodor's place and Leokadiya take some time to freshen up if she chose.

"I will take Sergei up to Fyodor's and be right back," was said quickly by Cynthia as she grabbed his hand and headed out the door ignoring the look's of her parents. When they got to the third floor apartment and Sergei opened the door with the key, she quickly pushed him into the entry and followed him inside.

"I am sure my father told you to be a gentleman and not to take advantage of his innocent daughter. My mother implied the same to me. That this should just be a friendship for now. I can agree with that, but just for now. This two weeks. But some day, maybe only in my dreams, I want to make love to you and I want you to make love to me. Not now, not here in Russia, but sometime, somewhere I want it to happen." She turned and walk out into the hall, closing the door behind her.

Chapter 11
2022

Page ten was blank. John was not surprised and was sure the expected telephone call from Mike tomorrow would tell him in person what would have been on it.

"How about we see what is being served for breakfast next door this morning?' was Allison's question asked with a subtle laughter in her voice. Having breakfast next door at Ben and Jennifer's house had become the custom for this group of new friends. The use of their home as the gathering space made a closeness that was valuable in their pursuit of bringing Rachmaninoff's lost works to the public.

They were three very similar houses, side by side, in a neighborhood of almost identical ones housing John and Allison, Ben and Jennifer, and Ed and Julia, right to left when viewed from the very ordinary Palm Desert street. But what was going on in those houses was most extraordinary.

John knocked on Ben's front door, then opened it, and he and Allison walked down the hall to the main living area. Whatever was being fixed in the kitchen that morning had the smells promising something very special.

"Haven't you left yet?" was Julia's friendly greeting, "Ben is fixing some French Toast this morning so go place your orders and service will be out by the pool as usual."

John and Allison thought no day could start better than this, although when they saw BJ and Cindy wander into the kitchen, looking a bit dazed, they both thought that some mornings for others could have started even better.

Out by the pool Ed was sitting in his usual chair, a nicely cushioned rattan design. Julia had brought out their plates and joined him sitting in a similar chair. A smile crossed his face as he surveyed the scene. It was a beautiful and comfortable Palm Desert morning now but in a few more hours the midday heat would have most of them back inside in the air conditioned houses. It was a nice backyard, the pool a right sized kidney shape with a dark bottom that seemed to give it a first class look. Good furniture and plenty of space to accommodate it.

They sat toward the shallow end of the pool and on a love seat midpoint to their right were BJ and Cynthia. BJ was the nickname that came early in his life as Ed and Julia had named their son Ben after his great-grandfather. Using Ben Junior quickly became BJ and that seemed to have become satisfactory to all. BJ's twin sister, Janice, was still attending college at UCLA finishing up working towards her Master's degree. Her live in boyfriend, at the kid's condominium, was doing the same and a wedding was thought to be a possibility in the near future. BJ's post graduate work had been curtailed because of whom he was sitting next to at the moment, so in love with her Ed could only hope it would be that way for the rest of his life.

It was very similar to his and Julia's start together, and it had happened in this same house. It had also been love at first sight and had him still totality in love with her. He hoped it would be for them as it has been for himself and Julia.

Looking at Julia he felt the same thrill he always did and thought the same thought that always came to his mind, "No one should be so lucky in life."

She was talking to Wilma who was in her special chair next to them and looked incredibly good and happy this morning, especially for a ninety five year old. She had found a large new family just when she was thinking she would have no one saying goodbye when that time came for her.

Ben and Jennifer were still in the kitchen fixing the last breakfast plates for themselves. They could be seen through the glass wall that showed off the kitchen from the pool, as it did the music room. Whatever had just been said, both were smiling. Ben had lost both his wife and his daughter, Julia's mother, to breast cancer when Julia was still in grade school and he became her parent. Ed's arrival came as Julia's college days were ending and Jennifer came into Ben's life as a visiting nurse about the same time.

John and Allison's chairs were of the same design and opposite to Ed and Julia's with their backs to the house. John's phone had just chirped and he spoke a few words and a look at Allison was all that was needed as he was off, wiping his mouth with a napkin and holding the phone to his ear. They had only been together for a few months but acted as if they had been together for years.

The only ones missing were Robert and Sandra who were at their house in Point Reyes Station, on the coast north of San Francisco. They were planning on being back here, staying at John and Allison's, next week.

Ed leaned back and stretched. It was all going so well for this group, the team, he could only hope it would continue that way for years to come. He was just thinking what he should do next when he felt Julia touch on his thigh. He looked at her and saw a smile that indicated maybe BJ and Cindy may not be the only one's in the group that had had the most enjoyable morning here in Palm Desert.

As John left Ben's front doorway he said his hello to Mike and page ten would be completed. Mike was in the Wauseon storeroom standing in front of the Steinway Parlor Grand Piano. It was on its legs, had been carefully covered with secured moving blankets and he was removing them as they spoke. It looked in remarkably good condition. He lifted the lid and positioned the strut to hold it in place.

"The letter C and the serial number below it shows 78754. The build is New York, not Hamburg as we were thinking. I will call them in a few minutes and see what we can find out about who bought it and where it was delivered. Before I do that, there are three taped up book boxes on a small pallet underneath the piano. Shall I take a quick look at one of those? Also one smaller box, also taped up, and there are seven banker boxes stacked against the wall."

"Open the smaller one. Is it about eighteen by twelve by eight?" John asked with excitement in his voice.

There was no answer from Mike as he knew from the question that was the one John wanted to see what the contents might be. John could hear the box being opened and then Mike picking up his phone. "Filled with what appears to be blank music sheets. There are a few that have some notations but don't seem to be organized in any way. Want them now?"

"No." was John's disappointed reply. "Do you have Steinway New York office on your phone?" John asked, but knew he needn't have.

Mike set up a third party line from his phone and punched the speed-dial. Moments later a friendly and professional voice answered from the New York Steinway Headquarters and the question on what can I do for you today was asked. Then, politely and efficiently, it was answered.

A Model C #78754 was a 1897 New York build and purchased by a Mr. Samuel Beckman of Cleveland, Ohio. It was shipped on November 11, 1897 to Saint Petersburg, Russia, 28 Zagorodny Prospekt, arriving and received by Mr. Beckman there and placed in his apartment on December 22, 1897, that date on the Julian calendar.

A thank you from both Mike and John was accepted and the young lady remarked that it was a very good, collectible piano and much sought after. She was sure they had a buyer at a very good price if they chose to sell it.

Chapter 12
2022

Ed and Julia did the clean up chores. They worked together in a well practice manner as they had since the day they met. First in golf when Ed had been brought into the family by Ben and two of his old friends, Hank Morgan and Morris Cornith. They both had retired from IBM as age and computer technology made the timing right. Ben retired and followed them out to Palm Desert a few years later.

Morris was wheel chair bound and designed and built golf clubs in his garage. He had never played golf but the one's he made had a magic for Ed. Hank and Ben had promised Morris's widow, at his funeral, that they would find someone who could play his clubs, get him on the PGA at the professional level and get Morris some recognition for all the time he had spent on creating and making them. It was Ed they found and he had been able to play in a number of PGA tournaments that first year. It was also how he met Julia on the first day he hit a golf ball with a Cornith golf club. Julia and Ed were together in Ben's house in the first week of their relationship and had been together ever since.

It was Hank's research on Ed's past that led to him seek out his mother's piano, have it restored and present it to him when the time was right. Hank had discovered that the reason Ed gave up his considerable talent as a pianist was because of the tragic death of both his parents in an horrific auto accident during his third year at Stanford University. He had been on a golf scholarship and had also been allowed the use of one of the music department's practice rooms when ever one was not being used. His mother, who was Vietnamese, had been his teacher and it was on her 1925 Steinway Model C piano that she had taught him not only how to play but how it should be played.

When the piano was shown to Ed in Hank's home, he was forced to reconsider what the direction of his life should be. At the same time Julia's past as a singer came to light and they formed Julia Renquest with Ed Adams. An excellent singer of popular songs, accompanied by an equally talented pianist. Their success as top entertainers covered over eight years until they decided their twins were more important to spend their time with than their music.

Ed, after the first years of parenting had been accomplished, started back on his road to classical music. It was his debut with the Los Angeles Philharmonic, just a few months ago, that set in motion John's attempt to make this last trip back in time.

John and his group of five Stanford drop-outs had decided, along with having to vacate their current space, that they had done enough traveling back in time. It was time for them to do the things they had post phoned and go their separate ways. Still friends and wishing the best for each other they closed down their enormous computer facility the night following Ed, Cindy and Allison's visit to Rachmaninoff.

It had been John's per chance attendance to the LA

Phil's concert that brought him into contact with Robert Johnson and Sandra Williams for the third time in the last nine years. He had joined them, or more accurately they had joined him, on a trip back in time of some 10,000 years to fulfill his childhood dreams of visiting the first natives settling in the San Francisco Peninsula. Robert had been his first time traveler and it was his choice, of the three visits he took with them, to visit Sergei Rachmaninoff. Seeing the two of them at the concert and their intense interest in Ed led to his following then into the donors party and overhearing Wilma Herman's claim of knowing Rachmaninoff when she had been a young girl. This is what had set the stage for this last great experiment in traveling back in time. How well it had gone had led to the formation this group of talented and interesting people gathered together in the three houses, side by side, in Palm Desert, California.

Chapter 13
1899-1900

Sergei stood perfectly still, staring at the closed door of Fyodor Chaliapin's apartment, not knowing what to do or think. The most beautiful woman he had ever met, only hours before, had made him a promise of what would happen between them that he would wait for, if necessary, the rest of his life. He knew that he would wake each morning wondering if it would be that day. The day did come but it would be ten years later and would be far from where he now stood, in a different time and circumstance.

Finally he moved and with his suitcase still in hand started an inspection of his friend's apartment. It seemed a bit small for such a big man as Fyodor. He was about the same height as Sergei but weighed at least fifty pounds more. None of those pounds were fat, but hard muscle that had been earned by his peasant beginnings. He knew hard manual labor but it was his deep and expressive bass voice that was carrying him to fame and fortune.

Just a year earlier he had married the Italian ballerina Iola Tornaghi and soon the first of their six children arrived. Another woman, Marina Petsold, a divorcee with two children, would later join him and soon three more daughters would be listed as his. The two families, one residing in Moscow and the other in Saint Petersburg, led separate lives but it would be many years later he would be divorced from Iola and then marry Marina. He was a bigger than life figure, both in personality and living, but he and Sergei were close friends for the rest of Fyodor's life. They were the same age and his death in April of 1938, at sixty-five, was five years before his best friend's would be in March of 1943.

Sergei found the apartment much to his liking. A big and comfortable bed, a closet with just enough space and two extra hangers to hang up his two shirts and his extra pair of trousers. The kitchen and dining room were fine but as it would turn out he wouldn't be using them that often. The bathroom was large and efficient. He took a look in the large mirror and his immediate thought was how could someone like Cynthia Beckman find him attractive. His next thought was did he smell as bad as he looked. He quickly changed into his best shirt, the better trousers and changed to his other shoes. A wash of hands, face and combing his hair had him make another inspection in the mirror.

Better, but not much. He didn't think he smelled too bad and thought he had no choice because that was the best he could do for now. He had at his mother's apartment several changes of clothes and some better shoes. Also underwear and socks. He even had his formal attire if need be. If he could make through tonight and tomorrow morning he would be okay the rest of his time on his stay here.

He left Fyodor's apartment and headed back to the apartment where there was someone he was falling in love with, without any understanding as how it could have happened and whether it was just some needed fantasy to keep him sane for one more day.

His knock was answered for him by the most beautiful woman in the world. She took his hand and pulled him into the room.

"You know Rimsky-Korsakov, don't you?" were Cynthia's first words to Sergei as he entered. They shook hands and said how good it was to see each other again. Nikolai said he would be seeing a lot of him over the next two weeks as he wanted to hear how his concerto number two was coming along. The handshake lasted about as long as the conversation and before Sergei could comprehend what had just happened he was out the door and gone from sight.

It was then that Cynthia started to laugh and took his arm to get him inside into her world with her parents and Leokadiya. They didn't to seem the least bit impressed by what had just happened. He hadn't embarrassed himself and it started to occur to him that maybe things would start to improve from the depth he had been in.

He was next listening to Leokadiya playing the first part of his Concerto 2 and she hadn't gone ten bars before he detected a very minor change in two chords that made an immediate improvement in the score.

Rose invited them to the table having some cheese wedges, sliced meats and breads presented with all the necessary condiments. Small plates, napkins and a glass of wine for each poured by Samuel. The food was good as was the wine. The conversation enjoyable and Sergei began to relax. Just a little.

Between bites Cynthia ask in a teasing manner, "Did you hear it? Tell us the truth."

Sergei looked at her, almost unable to speak, but came through with naming the exact notes that had been changed and that it played better than his original. He then said the right thing, "You two are going to save my life.

You have just held out your hands, taken mine and pulled me up from a place I don't want to be. I will never be able to thank you enough."

None at the table had anything to say to this but the look the two girls gave him made him feel he belonged here and with them. Even Rose smiled and Samuel had the look of a proud father.

Another hour was spent at the piano and a number of minor changes were in place when Samuel indicated that it had been a long day and that Sergei should take his leave. Cynthia and Leokadiya smiled acquiescence and he reluctantly made his exit. The look on Cynthia's face as he left told him she wanted to go with him but that she knew better and also that it wouldn't be happening in the next two weeks, either.

Sergei made ready for bed and slid in beneath the covers of a sheet and down comforter. He lay on his back staring at the dimly lit ceiling. He had never felt the desire for a woman more than he did for Cynthia at that moment. He could imagine the many that Fyodor had probably had here in this bed where he was laying. He didn't want anyone but her to be with him, but knew it wasn't going to happen. He closed his eyes and could see her smile, the shape of her mouth and smell the fragrance of her perfume. Sleep was not going to come easily and it would be hours before it finally did.

In a bed on the second floor below him there was a beautiful young woman having similar thoughts and desires. She was thinking of how it would be with him beside her and was silently sobbing into her pillow.

Chapter 14
1899-1900

The next morning Sergei woke tired, depressed and had a feeling of loneliness that was overwhelming. Getting out of bed seemed to be almost too much of an effort to accomplish. He dressed in the same clothes he had worn the last evening, shaved, washed and brushed his teeth. A look in the mirror what he saw didn't help his confidence or spirits.

He had had a long break from his April performance in London as a conductor and solo pianist to the day before yesterday performing his Fantasie for Two Pianos with Alexander Goldenweiser at the Large Hall of the Nobility. It was a mixed concert in which Fyodor had also taken part and it had gone well all though it did not pay them much.

He did some composing between the two events and the reception in London had been well received with them asking him to return the next season. He had even promised if he returned it would be with his Concerto Number 2 being on the program. It had progressed but only in the piano only format.

As he looked in the mirror he saw a poor soul who had accomplished almost nothing new in the last year and was broke. As usual his adopted Satin family had taken him in and paid some of his unpaid bills. And then Natalia had expressed what they both knew must be in their future just as he left to visit his mother in Saint Petersburg.

What had happened then, just a few minutes after boarding the train, could still not be imagined by who was looking back at him in the mirror. He could see the tears running down the checks of the sad face and saw the big hands reaching up to wipe them away.

One last look around and he left the apartment going down stairs. A few minutes later he was standing in front of the door that could lead him to salvation, or some thing that could be at least thought of as that.

He softly knocked on the door and waited. Hearing nothing, he knocked a little harder. Still no sound came from within but he couldn't move. He needed to see Cynthia if only to be sure she existed. He hoped he might not only be sure she was not a dream but might also have some time to lift his spirits before the long day he was to spend with his mother. Maybe Cynthia's mother would take pity and asked if would like some breakfast crossed his mind, this bringing a slight smile to his face as he thought he might still be alive.

It must have been five minutes before he could decide that they were not home and he retraced his steps back up stairs and change clothes to what he had worn on the train trip. He would walk to his mother's apartment building at 133 Fontanca River. It was about a mile and a half and it was a bitterly cold morning. At least it wasn't snowing and the gray sky was allowing a little sunlight to break through the gloom. The cold still made its way into his soul.

His mother, Lyubov Petrovna Butakova, had married young with a substantial dowry gifted from her father. Her new husband, Visily Arkadievich Rachmaninoff, had squandered most of it away by the time their fourth child, Sergei, had turned ten. She was twenty-two years old when he had been born and she would bear two more children. after him. Visily had always wandered about following his own desires and after their last estate had been seized by creditors, the family moved into the small flat that she still occupied but was now all alone.

It took Sergei almost an hour to get to her apartment and pressing the door bell had the door opened almost immediately. His mother had always looked at him with disapproval and a cold stare. For what ever reason she seemed glad to see him this time and he was hoping it would last for at least a few minutes.

It took only a minute for her to realize Sergei was shaking with cold, was thinner than she remembered him from his last visit months ago, and so forlorn looking she did something he was not expecting, giving him a gentle hug.

"How about we have an early lunch before you tell me every last detail about what is going on in your life. Something has happened and you should tell your mother all about it. Varvara has told me you still haven't got yourself back to form and writes she and Natalia are taking charge of your recovery. Tell your mother all about it as any good son would do." She had said this in a way Sergei didn't recognize. She seemed to actually care and he couldn't remember ever thinking that she had before.

Chapter 15
1899-1900

At the same time Sergei was knocking on their apartment door, Cynthia's father was introducing her and Rose to a young Russian executive he had been put in contact with by another businessman he had been working with over the last year. "A very smart young man you may want to listen to," was how he had been described to her by her father.

He was tall, maybe in his late twenties, and strikingly handsome by Russian standards. Cynthia's immediate thought was how could her father do this to her. She knew he didn't want her to be any where near Sergei without either her mother, or himself, not being close enough to know where and what she was doing with him. When her father asked how his wife and family were doing and he replied that they were doing fine and things were going nicely for them, she suddenly felt more at ease.

They were seated in a small French restaurant and as is usually the case eating at a foreign establishment often provides much better cuisine. As Sergei was slogging through the bitter cold morning towards his mother's apartment, his new family were enjoying the excellent croissants, condiments and coffee making for a delicious breakfast. The conversation then turned to business.

Rose was used to this and actually enjoyed how Samuel handled a meeting like this. It wasn't a sales, purchase or possible business proposition. It was a lively discussion of what was going on as the new century was about to start. It ranged from the telephone enterprise that was just underway to the increase use of fertilizer in farming and the equipment needed to spread it. They discussed the automobile and the parts that would be needed to make it work and the roads that were needed to make it useful.

At first Cynthia was bored, as her thoughts were elsewhere, but as the two men talked she became more and more interested in what was being said. It was not her world, nor would it be, but it was good that she knew there was another one and that it was important for her to know at least something about it. It would be the world she would be entertaining and she should have some knowledge about it if she was to properly entertain those in it.

Sergei downed the somewhat stale bread spread with butter and jam of an indistinguishable flavor. The ham was okay and had a good taste even with the chewing required to swallow it. His mother ate her servings without showing any care about its quality. There was little fruit this time of year and what was shipped in from other climates was very expensive so none was served. He, in any case, took seconds which his mother was pleased to see.

"Tell me what has just happened. Something has and I want to know every detail," was said in a manner that required an honest reply.

"Your sister and Natalia are planning my recovery with a second visit to Tolstoy and sessions with a Doctor Dahl that does some kind of hypnotherapy on depressed patients that seems to help. He lives in their apartment building and they are planning several months with me laying on his couch for an hour each day. I will have to try to stay awake as I seem to take a lot of naps of late."

Lyubov looked at her son with a sadness in her eyes she could not hide. He didn't notice, however, as he was looking off into his own world as he talked to her. She felt a guilt as this one truly gifted of her six children was not being able to follow his talent to deserved fame and fortune. He was a great pianist already, becoming known as a conductor of note and had already done compositions that demonstrated a skill few could match. He had now lost his confidence and was struggling to get it back.

She also knew something had happened, just recently, that had him thinking his problems were on the verge of leaving him by some other way than visits to other greats and some kind of subconscious massaging by a hypnotist.

"Who have you just met that has you thinking you are going to come out of this not needing help. I can sense it. Is it Natalia? Have you finally discovered she loves you and that you love her. Did she have to tell you after all these years you have been so close together. Is it that?"

His mother was saying all this in a voice he had never heard before. She was caring for him as he was and not for what he could be. She had always pushed him, many times much too hard and not caring of his feelings. He had never cried in front of her but the hurt had him in tears many times when he was alone.

"Yes, Natalia told me just as I was leaving for the train and I had been coming to the same conclusion. That she should be my companion as my wife and help me make the most of what I have to offer in music. But now someone else has entered my life. A love that happened yesterday morning not even a day after Natalia had come into focus. How can that happen, when it shouldn't have."

It was very quiet as Lyubov looked at her son as he sat across from her and she was searching for what to say. She had said things the wrong way to him so many times that she hesitated to say anything now.

.

Chapter 16
2022

John looked at Allison with the question on his face. She read it and responded, "It is time to bring Cindy in on what you are doing. Now is as good as any and our trip to Europe need not cause any problems. She has to know before another piano shows up."

It was the Friday before their Sunday flight so time was running out in that regard but it all could be delayed until they got back. John thought it best they talk to Cindy before they left as they planned to do some research with whatever they could find when at Senar. Allison was sure Cindy knew what they were up to so they might as well get things settled before they left for the two weeks they had planned.

That morning Ed and Cindy were seated together on the piano bench when John and Allison entered the music room. The obvious connection between the two had now become so accepted that no one was any longer questioning what it was. Two talents that had developed their own language to communicate, almost with out words. Ed and Julia had that communication when they were performing and still had it in their personal relationship. John understood what it was but had never been able to share it with another. Most people didn't even know it existed.

Cindy sensed their presence and turned to greet them.

"Are you going to let me in on your little secret before you head off to Europe?" she asked with a pleasant lilt that told them she already knew what was coming.

"We have found your Mother's piano, which is now yours, and want to know if you would like it here. There are also a number off other items you should have and we can store them for you to go through."

Allison first thought was that John had not done this correctly and was about to say something to that affect when Cindy solved her questioning John's approach.

"I think it is time we find out how I knew Sergei Rachmaninoff before I was born. I think I know and I am sure you do, or at least have a theory on how it happened. All we have to do is put the pieces together. Am I right?" Cindy's smile was radiant and all fears of it being a trouble for her had been put aside.

Ed offered the piano could be placed in their living area and it could be converted into a similar space as here in Ben's house. It would offer a place for her private practice. Ed could also use it for his and relieve some of the pressure of always having someone playing here in Ben's home.

They then sat together and John started explaining where they were going. Julia had walked in and joined the small group. BJ sat at Cindy's side, holding her hand.

"It looks like I will only be stating the obvious but sometimes that is the correct way to go about things. Cindy, you were told the stories of another person's relationship with Rachmaninoff. I think we can start with your great-grandmother Anne as the story teller. To have the ages correct it must have been her telling you the stories her mother had told to her. Here is what we have found out so far."

John paused with this and could see he had their interest, cleared his throat and told them of how his researcher had found the store room, paid the overdue rental and purchased the contents of the foreclosed on contents. It was legal and was in his name. The piano was identified and the record keeping of the Steinway company had given the name of a Samuel Beckman of Cleveland, Ohio the purchaser in 1897. The piano was delivered to an apartment in Saint Petersburg, Russia on December 22 that year, on the Julian calendar.

"Cynthia Beckman is a name I have heard of before. I can't remember when or where but I do recognize it. Do you think I was named after her? Was she a pianist? Had an affair with Sergei Rachmaninoff?" The questions came fast with no hesitation or sign of concern.

Allison was now smiling and John looked pleased as he was now certain Cindy had joined them in their search.

"We have the starting point and already have a little background to follow up with. At the address the piano was delivered to also lived Nikolai Rimsky-Korsakov and Leokadiya Kashperova," John said this while watching Cindy's reaction and was not disappointed.

"You have to be kidding me. Two of the top musicians of the time. Korsakov is well known by everybody and Kashperova, all pianist know her name now. An English researcher has just discovered her music scores hidden away in some vault in Saint Petersburg. Like our Library of Congress. He was doing research on Stravinsky and was trying to find out who had been the piano teacher he gave credit for bringing his skill as a pianist to the level of his compositions. He never gave her credit by name. What a great story and we will be part of it in a small way. A big way for me if not really so in the big picture. Graham Griffiths is the researcher. I think that's right."

Cindy's excitement was contagious and John now had the go ahead to do his research. This was his life, the search was what made it worthwhile. And he now had a partner that he could share it with who understood its importance to his own happiness.

Chapter 17
2022

The plans had changed a bit as one of John's old partners had called that morning and asked if his plans were still to fly to Paris on Sunday. How would he like to do the New York leg on Saturday in a private jet picking he and Allison up in Palm Springs at 10:30 for a three hour flight to New York. He and three friends were flying into Rome on Sunday morning. John accepted without asking Allison. She was delighted with this and would set up flying into Paris on an overnight leaving after their arrival in New York.

Within thirty minutes Allison had canceled the Palm Spring to New York reservation and changed it to a Saturday evening flight that had them to Charles DeGaulle by ten the next morning, Paris time. The reservations at the Hotel du Champ de Mars had the room available for the extra night and all was set.

John looked at Allison and they exchanged smiles. The relationship was working and the promise was that it would continue to grow. Tomorrow would be the start of another adventure.

Saturday morning Ed took them to the Palm Springs Airport and went in with them into the private plane terminal. Checking at the counter they were told their plane was expected in ten minutes and they would be aboard and off the ground in fifteen as no fueling was needed. It was as described and a handshake from John and a hug from Allison had Ed watching them, with their matching roller suitcases topped by smaller totes, head out to the gleaming Gulfstream IV. Allison had a shoulder bag and John a brief case. An attendant/co-pilot had the bags stowed and they entered the plane. Minutes later they were in the sky heading east.

It was a good flight and they were shuttled from a private airstrip to the JFK terminal and had about four hours to kill. The business class seats were comfortable and at just after noon local time, in Paris, they were sitting on the bed in the very nice and comfortable room at the Hotel du Champ de Mars.

The lady at the desk was a small woman in her late sixties, attractive and with a nice smile remarked on their Palm Desert address. John couldn't resist and asked, "Is there a boulangerie near by?" and her smile widened.

"Yes! It is on the corner and has been there for a hundred years. You must be friends with Ben Shea and Jennifer. I looked it up in our files. 1994 shows them here. A nice couple and have a nice story worth remembering."

After a needed rest in their room Allison suggested they take a walk down Rue Cler and check out the cheese shop, see if a small bottle of wine could be purchased and then head to the bakery. They were not disappointed and soon were sitting on a small bench with the Eiffel Tower being lit up as dusk descended on the Paris scene.

Jet lag in reverse had them wide awake until well after midnight and up just in time for the last call for the continental breakfast. The croissants were the best they had ever eaten with butter, special jams, fresh fruit and ex-cellent coffee had their day starting perfectly. Then they headed for the Louvre, for a very short visit. Fifteen euros seemed a reasonable price on Sunday but arriving about eleven was a mistake.

Directed to the Mona Lisa found a crowd eight deep with Allison only able to see her smile over the heads of several hundred bobbing about in front of her. John was only able to catch a glace of a portion of the famous painting between the shoulders of several people trying to extract themselves from the group in front of him.

There were people everywhere and they decided to find another part of Paris to explore. As if a magic hand had guided them on their exit they walked into the hall that had the Vermeer collection. It was not empty but a controlled movement allowed a close look at a number of his finest paintings. John, especially, thought it then had been worth the price of admission.

Outside they walked to the Place de la Concorde and then headed along the tree shaded walkway beside the Seine. It was a nice day so they made the circle around the Arc de Triumph, then down to the Eiffel Tower and back to the hotel.

A short visit to the room first and then a late snack at the nice restaurant across the street on the Rue Cler corner had them back to their room. The remaining cheese, a fresh baguette, peach and another small bottle of wine were taken on the same bench as the night before as the lights came on finished their first, full day in Paris.

Monday it was the fast TVG train trip to Lucerne. They had a good Swiss meal at the hotel about eight as their biological clock was beginning it's reset.

Chapter 18
2022

The Grand Hotel National Luzern provided them a fine room with an even finer view of the lake. They had the afternoon free so they took a leisurely walk around the area. A peek into the Casino was enough as neither enjoyed gambling.

Contact with the Serge Rachmaninoff Foundation seemed to have cooled a bit. The purchase by the Canton of Lucerne of the Villa and grounds had placed the Rachmaninoff Network that John had originally been contacted by in a undefined position as to who should be contacting him on his arrival.

The open house on June 18th and 19th had caused some confusion and Tuesday, the normal closed day, wasn't going to help. The performance of the matinee and evening performance of Rachmaninoff Number 7 in Palm Desert on the 18th had John's attention spread too thin and he was afraid he may have misunderstood how anxious the Foundation had been in seeing what they had.

A message at the hotel desk allayed his fears and a car would be waiting for him and Allison at 9:30 tomorrow morning to take them to the Villa. The weather was looking to be unsettled by noon so using the preferred open tour boat to bring them over was not a choice.

The car and driver, one of the staff of the Foundation, was there as promised and they had an enjoyable drive to Villa Senar. It was as described and the tour of the Villa and grounds was quick but thorough. It had been a very busy two weeks for the Foundation but it had been deemed a great success. It was Switzerland and they had not been disappointed.

There were three members of the Foundation to greet them and the initial talk was on the background of how the Rachmaninoff manuscripts had been discovered. John's rather vague presentation did not mention Cynthia, Ed and Allison's trip back in time and meeting Rachmaninoff, nor his recognizing Cynthia. Allison could only smile as John talked around this and admired how he had been able to do it so skillfully.

The high point, even more than the photos copies of the first three pages of the Concerto Number 7 manuscript was the copy of the brief notation in Rachmaninoff's own hand with "Is it possible for me to love two women at the same time? One is real and here all the time, the other comes and goes, but is always here when I need her. Look at what she wrote for me. How can I not love her?" message on the partial sheet having a beautiful melody of love.

One of the staff took the partial sheet to the big Steinway Grand, read it once and then played the eleven bars. He then played them again. The room was quiet and it seemed no one wished to break the silence.

It was left that the foundation would review the list of the contents of the three boxes of the Rachmaninoff papers that John's group had and might offer a way to do justice for them here at Villa Senar. It was of course not mentioned but everyone at the table, and all familiar with the subject, knew of the Sotheby's Music, Continental and

Russian Books and Manuscript auction in May of 2014 at which the 320 page Symphony Number 2 Manuscript met the gavel at £1,202,500.

It was left at that for now as there was a lot to think about and neither side was ready to make any decisions. It was a very impressive place. The Villa beautifully restored, decorated with a balanced collection of Rachmaninoff memorabilia and the grounds perfectly manicured. The Foundation staff were likewise most suitable in John and Allison's opinions and they left with the thought that it would be a good option if they chose that path.

As it was put by someone else, "These works do not belong in boxes under someone's bed."

It was raining hard as they were driven back to the hotel.

Chapter 19
1899-1900

Sergei looked at his mother. Something seemed different in her demeanor. Had she changed, or had he, was his first thought. She appeared sad and it was then he realized she was actually worried about him. It was something he had always thought she hadn't. For the first time in his life he began to realize it was possible that it was the way he had behaved that had caused her to be so critical and demanding of him as a child. That he had burdened her as to whether it had been her fault he hadn't succeeded at the Saint Petersburg Conservatory. When he was twelve years old he was placed with his mother's sister in Moscow and made his name there at the Conservatory.

The family's descent into poverty as his father frittered away his mother's dowry, forcing them into the small apartment where he was now sitting was not really understood by the younger ones at the time, including Sergei. Then the deaths of two of his sisters, Sofia at age twelve and Elena at twenty, had further sent her into depression which was now becoming understood by him and he decided he needed to do better by her from now on.

"Her name is Cynthia Beckman, an American that has been here in Saint Petersburg for three years with her mother and father. They speak Russian fluently and several other languages as well. She is beautiful, an excellent pianist, has been taking lessons from Leokadiya Kashperova and they are good friends. They live in the same apartment building as Rimsky-Korsakovs. I fell in love with her at first sight." Sergei got all this out in one breath.

Lyubov smiled, a real and loving smile, and started to gently laugh at her forlorn son. "Sergei, Sergei how gullible you still are. Did you learn nothing from the Skalon sisters. Little Vera teasing you, letting you hold her hand. Her sisters egging you on while her mother went crazy with worry you would soil her precious little girl."

Sergei sat very still looking at his mother as she made fun of him in a good way. He was actually enjoying it. He had written letter's addressed to Vera's oldest sister, as he had be forbidden to write to her, for many years all to learn that Vera had another boy friend at the time. She would marry him without ever having told him about her true love.

"I met the Beckmans yesterday morning. They had attended my performance the night before and Cynthia had seen me enter the economy carriage. She made her father come back and get me to share their first class compartment for the trip. I met Leokadiya for the first time as she was also their guest." Sergei got this off in the same manner as his first introduction of his new interest. And then he continued, "We spent the long day on the train and the two girls started to look over my piano concerto number two scoring. They both could sight read and liked what I had written. It was the second and third movements first, and then they started on the first which has me in despair. I can't describe to you how much this has helped me already. Then after we got to the apartment and having a light meal, we continued on her piano. A beautiful Steinway small grand. The evening ended with Cynthia walking me to Fyodor's apartment and telling me she wanted to make love to me but not now and not here in Russia. Sometime later, some other place but she wanted me to make love to her."

"Oh you poor little boy. How could such a thing happen to you now with Natalia just telling you the same thing but without any mention of place or time. How long are the Beckmans going to be here?"

"They are going back to America before the end of January. I have to be back in Moscow by the ninth." Sergei answered with a sadness in his voice.

"You know what is the right thing to do. I don't need to tell you anything. She is absolutely right, not here and not now. Honor that!" was his mother's advice.

They talked about many things over the next few hours and much to Sergei's surprise he enjoyed being with his mother for a change. She casually mentioned she was just sixteen when Elena was born, then Sofia and Vladimir came next. He was born when she was twenty-two and that was the age his new love was now. Arkadiv was next and the last of his siblings, Varvara, was born when she was thirty-one. By that time his father was getting most of his satisfaction in other places but not in their bed.

Sergei confided for what ever reason he was starting to think better of himself and was hoping his time with Cynthia and Leokadiya would get his concerto composition to the point of doing the tweaks and minor improvements that were always necessary. He felt he would be able to approach the orchestration next. He had hope for his future for the first time in several years.

Just before heading back to whom and what was waiting for him on Zagorodny Prospect, he asked his

mother if she would like to be invited to one of the gatherings that Kashperova and Rimsky-Korsakov had on Tuesday and Wednesday evenings. He could walk over and
they could either walk back or get a carriage.

"You're broke again, aren't you Sergei?" and she
gave him ten rubles. "If you can arrange it I would love to
met your new friends. I have met Nadezhda and Nikolai a
few times but they won't remember me except as your
mother. It would be fun and I need something like that in
my life right now."

Sergei had a pleasant walk back to the apartment
and there was even some sunshine on the path.

Chapter 20
1899-1900

Sergei went to Fyodor's apartment and changed into the fresh shirt and trousers he had brought back from his mother's place. He washed his face and neatly combed his hair. It was then, with the best intentions to control his emotions, he headed to the Beckman's apartment. He could hear the piano was being played so knocked firmly on the door.

The piano music stopped and it was Cynthia who opened the door and all his good intentions of not letting his emotions overcome his reasoning left him completely. She smiled and he did his best to smile back and managed an awkward, "I am back."

Cynthia pretended not to notice and took his hand and led him over to the piano. Leokadiya was sitting on the far end of the bench, gave him her best smile and asked, "Are you ready to hear what we have done to your first movement?"

"Don't worry Sergei, just a few changes. Cynthia, you do the honors," she continued, then standing saying she needed to go upstairs for a few minutes and would be right back to find out what Sergei thought of what they had done.

Cynthia then sat down in the player's position and Sergei sat next to her to the right. The marked up score was on the stand and was on sheet six beginning at bar fifty-four. She knew the start and played flawlessly through until she reached the bars with a number of changes and then on through them. Sergei recognized the improvement immediately. It wasn't enough to be that noticeable but it was much better. She moved aside and he played through and passed through it, including the changes, without looking at the score.

She was sitting close to him and watching the expression on his face as he finished. She could see the concentration and knew he liked what they had done. He turned to look at her and before he could say a word he bent to her and kissed her on the lips. A long kiss that she accepted and when he pulled away he said, "I shouldn't have done that. I promised your father I wouldn't but I can't help myself. I feel helpless."

The door had opened and Leokadiya was back and could see she had timed it just right. She and Cynthia had planned to have him play through the score and find out if he would accept the changes in the good intended manner they had been made. Also, if Cynthia was correct on how he would behave if they were alone together. His apology and acknowledgment that Cynthia's father had spoken to him had been established and she was comfortable with that although not happy about the outcome. He would be going back to Moscow in two and a half weeks and she could not afford to risk more than a few days before the end of this week to be any closer than a kiss like the one she had just received. He was the first man she had ever had this immediate desire for and felt her mother was right in not allowing herself too much liberty with him. She would stand by what she had said to him last night, not now, not here in Russia, but sometime, somewhere it would happen.

Just then the door opened and Rose and Samuel entered with several bags of groceries and invited their two guest to stay for dinner. Sergei was thinking he had gone to heaven and Leokadiya knew she was there.

It was a fine dinner of meat, potatoes and vegetables cooked American style and the desert was cake from a nearby bakery run by a young Swiss baker named Walter Huber. Samuel had struck up a good relationship with the somewhat bashful youngster constantly teasing him about courting the Russian lovelies. He never mentioned he had a daughter about his age, however.

After dinner the concerto number 2 for piano was played by Sergei, start to finish, including all the changes, for the first time. Forty-four minutes with a few more spots noted along the way for maybe changing. Sergei played from memory and it was flawless. All five there understood what had just been heard and what was going to be it's reception. In symphony form, it could only be imagined but they knew what it would be like.

Sergei Rachmaninoff now had a secret he would never share with anyone. He would visit Tolstoy and he would lounge on Dr. Dahl's couch for as many sessions as others thought necessary. He would use that time to dream of other music to be composed, of those who had helped him, and about one in particular that he would meet somewhere else in time when the time was right.

Chapter 21
2022

The forecast for the rest of the day was for more light rain. John and Allison had brought one small umbrella and walked under it a short distance from the hotel until they found a small restaurant that was serving early. There were several empty tables and a quick appraisal of the highlighted fondues on the menu made it seem a good choice.

After an appropriate delay the chef, in a starched white apron and cap, approached them and asked in rather good English if they had found something they would like, pointing at the menu they were sharing. It was all in German and French and although John could read both he posed would the Chef pick out the one he thought they would like the best.

John had asked this in as close to the dialect he was hearing at nearby tables and the Chef immediately lost his aloof mannerism and suggested their specialty that creates the good mood that fondue is known to provide. John smiled at this and asked the Chef to serve it with a wine that would make their good mood even better. A bow was taken and the chef was off to the kitchen.

The chaffing dish was presented with a basket of bread chunks, two plates and two fondue forks. The smell was right, the wine correct and the flavors outstanding. After the first few pieces of bread were dipped and eaten the Chef beamed and spoke to John in a secretive manner that it was the custom that if he knocked his lady's bread off her fork as she swirled it in the cheese she was obliged to let him kiss her.

John promptly did this and then explained to Allison what had been said to him. She didn't hesitate and pulled John to her giving him a solid kiss at the same time as knocking the bread off his fork. The wine was excellent and the fondue was enjoyed.

Gelato was next and it took several minutes to select the flavor from the twenty-four flavors offered. They shared a cone, the rain had stopped and the sunset over the lake was beautiful. Their mood was definitely good.

On the walk back to the hotel a travel agents window display advertised three days in Venice with travel by train taking less than five hours time from Lucerne. Allison pulled John over to the window and announced that three days in Venice sounded good to her and they should go.

As things always seem to happen as John talked to a hotel desk clerk about train service to Venice, he pointed out the train station in view around a corner of the lake and offered that the station in Venice was in the middle of the tourist area. He then, of course, mentioned a second cousin that had a very nice bed and breakfast just off San Marco Square.

Within ten minutes the reservations were made, they would keep their room at the hotel and travel light with one case and a tote bag. Wednesday morning they boarded the train with good seats with window views. It was a spectacular ride though the mountains, down over the country side and then into the center of Venice. A water taxi ride had them three blocks from the B & B and the room was as promised.

By four o'clock that afternoon they were strolling, holding hands, wandering through the streets and walking over the small bridges crossing the myriad of small canals. "You can't get lost, your on a island," John said and fifteen minutes later they were lost.

Allison squeezed John's hand and announced, "I think this has put me in a very good mood. How is your mood right now?"

Chapter 22
2022

It was a very pleasant evening, a stand up dinner at a Trattoria with an exceptionally fine menu, and then off for another decision to make at a gelato bar. The B & B was a good recommendation with a nice, quiet room, queen size bed and a fine bathroom. Their first night in Venice was just as John had hoped for. Allison seemed especially happy as they snuggled up for the nights rest. Their morning was also very nice as was the breakfast.

San Marks square was reached early by another water taxi ride but was already getting crowded. They were lucky and toured the Basillica seeing the original bronze horses inside but skipped the Doges Palace and escaped the square leaving just enough space for two more tourists to reach the square's maximum capacity.

Leaving the crowd behind they wandered about with no plan in mind. They found many of the best tourist sites and enjoyed visiting several if there were no lines. It was that afternoon, when after short visit to the B & B for a break, their real adventure was about to begin. Walking into the nearby Campo San Maurizio had them in front of the Museo della Musica. Going in it was a thrill of a lifetime for Allison. John's pleasure came from what was there and how Allison's reaction to it played out. Case after case of the fine instruments of the past. Violins, cellos, bases, some collections of wind instruments, and the earliest pianos. It was in an old church converted for its purpose with the altar displaying instruments and chairs ready for a performance.

The attendant noticed them as there were few others looking around and none showing the interest and concentration of Allison's. He eventually walked over and asked her, in passable English, whether she played. Allison replied that she did play the piano and the attendant asked them to come with him.

In a side display was the shop where some of the restoration techniques were displayed and some actual work was being done. Against the back wall was a large piano somewhat the size and shape of a grand. Only fifty-six keys but still in an octave arrangement.

"We are not sure who built this piano. It had to be in the late 1700 or early 1800s. It is the oldest of the long string pianos and plays quite nicely. Would you like to play something?" was asked of Allison and John thought he had never seen someone as excited as she looked at that moment. A chair was positioned for her and she gently pressed the middle octave keys. Then in the above and below. The sound was beautiful and not far from what would be heard on a modern piano. There were no pedals but she could accommodate for that by adjusting how long she held a key down.

She played the two pieces Cindy had composed and that she had memorized. Several tries had it as it should sound and she continued avoiding any parts that went outside what she had available on the key board.

It turned out the attendant was the manager of the entire museum. He was a tall and handsome Italian in his forties and was obviously enjoying guiding Allison. She, in John's eyes, had never looked better with her excitement at the privilege of playing this special piano bringing a nice look and color to her face.

"I would like to invite the two you to a social function we have every Wednesday evening at my house. I have a modern grand piano and no piano player this evening. If you, turning and smiling at Allison, would like to play for your, and your partner's, dinner tonight I think you would find it fine time." He had a great smile and Allison almost answered but first turned to John.

John was enjoying everything that was happening and answered to the affirmative in perfect Italian. Alberto Depolo smiled even more broadly and the instructions of time and place resulted in meeting him at the front of the museum at seven and he would take them by boat to his home. He was sure they would have a fine evening with his wife and their friends. Dress was casual but if they had brought a little less casual outfit they might be more comfortable.

The boat ride was more than just to his home but a scenic ride in the Grand Canal just as the evening lights were coming on. They docked at a private dock and entered the Depolo home that was like a House Beautiful magazine cover. Mrs. Depolo, Anna, fit the scene and the small group of two dozen of their closest friends were there. French, English, Italian and some Russian were being spoken in a variety of combinations.

After too many introductions to be remembered Alberto escorted Allison to the big grand piano and she took a seat and ran her fingers over the keys. John was amazed how beautiful she looked and at her confidence which added to that beauty. She didn't seem to have any doubts about playing this enormous piano with a sizable group of obviously sophisticated people crowded about.

She immediately played Cindy's two pieces and instantly everyone there knew they were hearing something very special. John had been so busy with his own part in the Rachmaninoff unveiling that he hadn't realized how much time she had been practicing on her own. She then played the second movement of Rachmaninoff 2 and then played the third movement of the just found number 7.

Most of the attendees realized they had never heard this last piece and the questions started. John was busy with the interpreting and their hosts seemed delighted on how things had turned out. Dinner was served and it was an elegant meal served on a long table that Allison and John had only seen the likes of in the movies.

About midnight the group broke up with the comments of the best ever party attended as the main conversation and all hoped that they would see each other again. The boat trip back to the dock near the museum's square was an event of its own as all the big homes along the Grand Canal were lit up inside to show off the main rooms. It was a fairyland of palaces and the close of one best days of Allison and John's lives.

When they made into their bed at the B & B they looked at each other and started laughing. Allison said it best, "My God John, how do you get such things to happen. It is magic and I am having so much fun I can't wait for what you bring into my life next."

Chapter 23
1899-1900

It was early the next morning as Sergei lay awake in his bed knowing that Cynthia Beckman was in a bed in the apartment just one floor below him. He had never had this strong of a desire for a woman before and it seemed for him to be not only emotionally, but physically, painful. Thinking his desires for her may be satisfied sometime in the future was of no help at the moment. He was pretty sure of what his future held for him and it would make it almost impossible for him to ever know what it might be like to have her with him. Would he ever feel like this toward Natalia? Was it even fair for him to have such a thought?

The cold shower he took didn't help, as he knew it wouldn't. The long walk in the bitter cold and gray morning with the stale pastry and tasteless coffee for his breakfast made things even worse. As he entered the apartment building he met Samuel exiting and was invited to walk over to a different bakery to pick up some fresh bread for making french toast at their place this morning. Would he he like to join them was asked and quickly accepted.

When they arrived Leokadiya was also there and she and Cynthia smiled their good mornings. Sergei's outlook for the day became much improved.

Igor Stravinsky was expected by Leokadiya for his daily lesson at her apartment but she said he often came early in hopes, as he did this morning, to be invited to breakfast. He was lucky this morning. He was seventeen years old and thought not only was he much more mature than that age but that he should be welcomed just by his mere presence. He was invited to breakfast but Samuel and Rose knew how to skillfully steer the conversation towards the others instead of just about him. Even with this, Sergei Rachmaninoff thought he was in heaven. He also thought that the french toast had also come from there.

Leokadiya took Igor away for his lesson in her apartment and Cynthia was laughing quietly as they left. She was now having her lessons with Leokadiya as playing lessons. She would memorize certain scores and be critiqued as she played. They were also composing together as teacher and student and now had together this new project in saving Sergei from himself and the first movement of his Concerto Number 2. Samuel and Rose thought they had struck a very good deal in choosing Kashperova and by renting this apartment for their stay in Russia. Sergei would get a better understanding of this in the next two evenings, as a guest at Leokadiya's Tuesday and Rimsky-Korsakov's Wednesday social gatherings.

He would be surprised by being treated as a featured guest at both events. This was all starting to bolster his confidence and bring real happiness into his life again. He looked at Cynthia as she helped her mother clean up the breakfast clutter but didn't notice that Samuel had caught his look. When Sergei stood and offered his help, two good things happened, neither of which meant as much to him then as it would later, much later. The smile from both Cynthia and her mother on his offer with their refusal and a look, not of approval but of acceptance, from her father.

The morning was spent with the three young people working on the first movement. It was quickly improving and Sergei was already composing the orchestration of sections in his mind. Composing was coming back to him as it had been before. Even better, as heard portions being played by Cynthia and Leokadiya calling out the bars he was imaging the instruments and how to score them as he heard the piano's voice speaking to him.

The time had flown by with Samuel seeming able to handle his work even with all the piano and talking going on by the three musicians. Rose was reading another book and Sergei's quick glance at the title had surprised him as it was Russian history and in a Russian print. He asked her about the title and she smiled, saying something to the effect of what a troublesome past his country had been through, but added that so had America.

What she said next was said in a rather carefully structure sentence. "I think the past here is about to repeat itself and you should be thinking on how you can protect those near to you that are worth you protecting." The sadness briefly showed on her face, then disappeared as fast as it had been shown. She went back to her reading without saying, or offering to say, anything more.

A light lunch was served and then the girls suggested a walk and that they should visit Sergei's mother and invite her to the Wednesday night gathering at Rimsky-Korsakov's. Leokadiya thought she would have a better time with the older crowd that came there than the youngsters at her gathering.

It was a much nicer afternoon than the morning had been and the sun shown brightly through the gray sky.

Cynthia's Dreams

Sergei was a little doubtful about this impromptu visit, especially with him having to introduce Cynthia without his mother knowing immediately what was happening between them. Neither of them had any qualms about this and Sergei also wanted to involve his mother into his life again. She had made the choice to stay in Saint Petersburg when he was sent to Moscow to attend the Conservatory there. It had left her alone after the deaths of two of her daughters and the military taking her other two sons.

The walk went better than good as the two girls took charge walking on either side of Sergei, each taking an arm, and bumping against him in a teasing manor. At six foot three, having the rather tall Cynthia on one side and the shorter Leokadiya on the other they kept him off balanced most of the way. Each discussed how he would be treated if either of them caught him alone.

The four long blocks to Sergei's mother's apartment building went quickly. Their visit took longer than expected but went very well. The two girls acting in such a friendly way toward her soon relieved some of his concern but it was obvious there was such an attraction between Sergei and Cynthia that Lyubov couldn't miss it. She had had much experience with young love as she was only twenty-two, as was Cynthia now, when she had born Sergei, her fourth child. Her first daughter was born when she was just sixteen.

Wednesday at Rimsky-Korsakov's was eagerly accepted by Lyubov. Sergei would come to get her and they would walk back together. She was only fifty-nine and walked all over Saint Petersburg as needed in her everyday life. If the weather was bad a carriage could be hired.

Chapter 24
1899-1900

Saturday night for Sergei was as it had been the night before, but sleep did come and the next morning went better. He didn't know that Cynthia was having those same feelings and was having trouble coping with him being so close and not being able to be with him.

It was six days until Christmas day for the Beckman family. They were very traditional Americans on this holiday and December 25 seemed, even on the Julian calendar, preferred to the actual day, January 7, in Russia. Also, Cynthia's Model C Steinway piano had arrived on December 22, 1897 as her surprise Christmas present and made that Christmas so special they would keep December 25, while here, as the date to celebrate.

Leokadiya and Cynthia were preparing for some decorating of her apartment for the gathering tonight and preparing the platters for the expected twenty people coming. The guests were expected to bring their own drinks, other than water, and items to be shared for eating. It was generally young people, many Conservatory senior students and a few local musicians trying to make ends meet in an competitive field. There were almost always a violinist and cellist, bringing their instruments up to the fifth floor and they were always offered some time to entertain. Several pianists would play Leokadiya's piano, sometimes with a new composition to debut.

Cynthia's Dreams

Sergei had some time alone in the Beckman's apartment as the girls were running up and down getting things ready and Rose and Samuel were out doing some shopping on their own. He liked Cynthia's Steinway Model C piano as the touch was every bit as good as on the best grand pianos. The sound was also excellent, even in the small room.

He played through the first movement of number 2 twice, smiling in relief at how close it was to matching what he was wanting it to be. Concerto Number 2 for piano was ready. Scoring for the orchestra was already done for 2 and 3 and 1 was now complete in his mind. He only had to put it on paper and he would be ready hear it on the big stage. A Symphony version would complete the works and he was now confident it would happen. "Merry Christmas to you, Sergei Rachmaninoff," he said to himself.

Cynthia had come down from upstairs and as the door had been left ajar she walked in without Sergei seeing her. He was just finishing the first movement and she could see that he was satisfied with it. She waited and couldn't decide whether to go back up to Leokadiya's or make her presence known. Sergei solved that by turning around and seeing this beautiful young women staring at him. He smiled and motioned for her to come sit by him on the piano bench.

As she sat down he started to play the second of the two works she had composed and played though about a third when he nodded to her and played it slightly different. "That is better, Sergei. Just those few notes. Let me get my score and we can make those changes right now," and she was off to her room coming back with the box of sheet music. Pulling out the six pages, three each for the two compositions she wanted, and placed them on the music rack.

With eraser and pencil she changed the half dozen notes in the two bars Sergei had played differently. He was pleased she had recognized each note he had changed when playing and had entered these correctly. He played through the piece start to finish and nodded that it was as it should be.

Cynthia wrote on the top of the first page of each, 1899 Cynthia, placed the six sheets together and handed them to Sergei. "These are for you. You can use them, play them, or just keep them hidden away. I want you to have something of mine to remember me by." Her tears started to come and Sergei reached for her, brought her face to his and kissed her. It was a kiss he would remember the rest of his life and when she pulled away he watched as she went to her room and closed the door. He could hear her crying and could not keep his own tears from falling on the pages he was holding.

He went upstairs and placed the precious music sheets in his folder.

Chapter 25
2022

The next morning John and Allison lay in bed not wanting to get up. Last night was an event they knew would seldom be matched again. John was so proud of Allison he didn't have the words to express his feeling accurately. A loss for words which was not something he was used to having.

"You are lost for words, aren't you?" was asked by Allison as she rolled up against him and continued, "You little rascal, I think I am in love with you. How have you managed to do that to me?" she said with laughter in her voice. John still couldn't say a thing and just smiled at her. He would get around to expressing his love for her when the words he needed came back to him.

It was decided that today they make the effort to get lost in Venice. After the nice breakfast they took care of what was needed and then headed out crossing the Grand Canal over the Accademia bridge into the Campo Santo Stefano and with no real destination crossed the Canal again over the famous Ponte de Rialto. They had wandered north and ended up crossing the pedestrian bridge to the railway station. Another crossing had them walking back across the Rialto and in another hour they found themselves taking another peek into Piazza San Marks but not trying to enter into the mob that had filled it wall to wall. Finding a small trattoria for an early lunch and then headed back to the B & B.

A short rest and John said he would like a return visit to the music museum and they were there in fifteen minutes. Alberto was at his post and gave them a handsome Italian man's smile. A handshake for John and a kiss on the cheek for Allison.

"I have someone for you to meet a second time. He was at our dinner last night but always hangs back a bit and observes. He is an excellent observer. He told me he would like to talk to you if you came in today." Alfredo took them back to the restoration area and they were introduced to Gouvanni Santio. He was sitting at one of the big tables carefully stringing what appeared to be an old, but totally restored, violin.

He was late in life but had clear, bright eyes and the smile he gave John and Allison was radiant. "I am glad you stopped by as I have a story to tell you about my grandfather Benedetto." He smiled again and tightened the last string and plucked it. A few more adjustment were made, then he plucked the four strings making a few more adjustments and finally set the violin on a pillow and smiled again.

"We think it maybe a Vincenzo Cavani of about 1910. Maybe a bit older. It looks the same but doesn't have any markings that make a sure identification. Do you play?" he asked, looking at Allison.

"A little. I practice now and then but mainly I am a pianist," was Allison's answer.

Gouvanni picked up the violin and handed it to her with the bow that was laying next to the pillow. "Would you like to be the first person to play a violin that hasn't been played in a hundred years. It spent all that time, in disrepair, in an old family chest handed down generation after generation. It was bought by the museum in a lot auction ten years ago and I have spent the last year slowly restoring it. I don't work so fast anymore and the museum is okay with that."

Allison was hesitant but her expression showed she wanted to play it and John watched as she quickly positioned the instrument under her chin, adjusted her hand and lightly plucked the strings. She placed the bow gently tapping the strings feeling the pressure. Bowing a few times had the wonderful sounds of a quality violin and before either John, or Gouvanni, said anything she started Vittorio Momti Csardas, a popular Italian folk piece.

Alberto had gone out to greet a group that had just entered and as the music floated out into the museum he steered them over to the window that showed the restoration area of the display and they watched and listened as this tall woman confidently played this spirited Italian favorite.

Allison had made some minor errors but covered them by continuing playing without showing any hesitation or embarrassment. Gouvanni couldn't suppress his pleasure of what he was hearing and led the applause when she had finished.

"I use to play this piece on the piano with a violinist friend and after practicing we would exchanged instruments. I became a better violinist and she a better pianist. I only know about five pieces and this is the one I can play best. It is a marvelous violin Gouvanni and you have done such a good job." Allison handed the violin back to him along with a hug and a kiss on his cheek.

He smiled and then said, "Now, let me tell you a

story. My grandfather, as a very young man, had been a favorite piano tuner for Steinway Pianos and was offered a job in New York. It was a chance for him to go to America and they had paid for his trip from here. His father was Italian, his mother was a Russian and he could speak both languages and English good enough to understand and speak it. He had been over there about two years when Rachmaninoff made his first American Tour. He had specified he would like a Steinway Model D for his performances and wanted a full time tuner to travel with him. This was from the end of October of 1909 until the end of January 1910."

Gouvanni took a short break, then a sly smile came over his face. "This is about something no one knows about and it could be I shouldn't be telling you about it now. Last night you played two pieces that were not Rachmaninoff but that I have heard before."

Both John and Allison abruptly looked up at Gouvanni and he could see he had been right. The two pieces were not by Rachmaninoff but were so close they had to have been composed by someone close to him. He knew who it had been and he could tell John and Allison also were thinking they knew who it was. His grandfather had known her, and loved her in his own way. "Cynthia Beckman was her name. Am I right about that?" he said letting the question hang in the air.

Allison broke the silence, "We would like to know how you know this. You are right. She was the composer and we are, with a few others, trying to find out how it could have happened. There is much more as to why we are interested in this as we have a young pianist that is convinced she had spent time with Rachmaninoff, composed those pieces with him, and can play them. Not only that but much better than I did last night."

Gouvanni sat back in his chair with what had now become a permanent smile. He then told them how it had happened. "My grandfather was sworn to secrecy so, as I just told you, I am not sure I should even be telling you this. He was on his death bed when he told me of the beautiful lady that had joined them in New York City at the start of the tour in November of 1909. She would have a hotel room at every stop on the tour and had one in New York. They were very discrete and if ever caught off guard would have her introduced as his secretary, manager and interpreter. According to my grandfather they were totally in love with each other. He said Rachmaninoff treated her as well as any woman could be treated. When the tour ended they went their separate ways. He told my grandfather he was afraid that both their hearts would break."

Cynthia Beckman now had her place in the story. John's researcher had found out she had a child in the later part of 1910. They now had the link they had been looking for.

Chapter 26
2022

Alberto, Gouvanni, Allison and John stood together in the restoration room and said their thank yous and goodbyes. Gouvanni received a very grateful second hug and kiss on his cheek from Allison which he seemed quite pleased with. Alberto walked them to the front of the museum and received his a hug and kiss from Allison and an envelope from John. He thanked them both and put the envelope in his pocket.

He went back to the small kiosk he sat in as he waited for visitors and with none in sight, opened the envelop. A $10,000 donation drew a smile and he placed the check into a bank deposit envelope. It was more than a typical months donations by the walk-in visitors. It was such a nice museum, and one of the few with free admission. He always thought they should have many more visitors than they did but felt the free admission was valued by all that had visited. Those fortunate enough to have come inside would always remember the museum as a highlight of their visit to Venice.

John and Allison had hit their limits. Last nights dinner and socializing combined with more walking than usual, along with the remarkable event at the music museum, had them ready to lay down and close their eyes for a few minutes. Keyed up by the knowledge that Cynthia Beckman had an almost three month affair with Rachmaninoff and that he must have been the father of the child she bore around nine months later had established the link to Cindy's thinking she had been with him back in time. It was easy to visualize baby Cindy in her great-grandmother's lap being rocked to sleep while hearing the love stories her mother had told of the time she had spent with Sergei Rachmaninoff.

"It is a nice story to think about, Cindy being told the stories of a great-great-grandmother's past with him." Allison said this as John had looked her way and he could see how emotional this was for her. He reached out to touch her shoulder and could see her tears starting to fall. He moved closer and gently kissed her.

"How much was the donation you gave to the muesum, five thousand?" Allison wasn't going to fall apart about her thoughts about little Cindy and John just answered, "Twice that."

"That sounds right by me. That is some museum and what it contains is more than just a bunch of old violins. I wonder if Gouvanni's latest renovation might be for sale?"

"I will find that out. I would think it might be as that year and maker is already in their collection. Let's make one more visit before we leave tomorrow morning." As John told her this the smile he was expecting shown on Allison's face.

The next day as they headed for the train station Allison was proudly carrying an old violin case with an even older violin inside. The bow was also there and was the same one she had used on the first playing of the violin. John, but not Allison, also knew how special it was.

They arrived in Lucerne and since they had kept

the room they only had to pick up the key and go upstairs. As soon as they were in the room Allison took out her violin, positioned it and played a small romantic piece for John. She then gave him a little more in the way of a most enjoyable thank you.

Spending three more days in Paris they made one more try at the Louvre at the opening and raced the rest to Mona Lisa to pay their respects. For John it was his first chance to receive her smile and he felt it was well worth the hassle.

The flight back on Wednesday with a good connecting flight had them back in Palm Desert before sundown with their biological clocks messed up again.

As they entered Ben's house they could hear the sounds of Rachmaninoff Number 5 and entering the music room they saw Cynthia Anne Ashbaugh at the piano never looking more beautiful. Ed was standing nearby, watching her play this magical piece, with adoration in his eyes. Julia, Ben and Jennifer were seated in the big chairs and Wilma and BJ were sitting together on the small couch.

They sat in two of the empty chairs and waited until the third movement had ended before the hellos and welcome backs were taken care of.

Chapter 27
1899-1900

The plans for Leokadiya's gathering suddenly got more complex. Nikolia Rimsky-Korsakov had decided that since Sergei was a guest of honor and that they did not have a piano they should combine the gatherings. The decision was made to hold both Tuesday and Wednesday evenings at Leokadiya's, and hope the quests would not overlap too much.

It started out well. A small group of six Conservatory students came promptly at eight, went directly to the appetizers and then with small plates filled began their introductions and how nice it was to meet Leokadiya and Sergei. Stravinsky was there and had started to play first. It was on the demanding side and Leokadiya suggested he let Sergei have some time at the piano.

Cynthia stood with her parents and as soon as Sergei was seated on the piano bench she positioned herself on the curved side of the piano so she had the best view. He smiled at her and played one of her compositions with such compassion that every one in the room could, even if not seeing, sense the connection they shared with this piece of music.

Just as he had finished there was some confusion in the doorway and a very young couple were struggling into the room with a cello case. Cynthia's father went to their aid and managed to make space enough by the piano for brother and sister Munous, Kirk and Claire, to position themselves with their instruments. They were welcomed and introduced themselves. They were here from England for a one year attendance at the Conservatory. Their teacher had suggested they might enjoy meeting Leokadiya and if they could get their instruments up to her apartment that evening she may ask them to play. It was almost like a joke was being played on Leokadiya as they were both small and looked hardly old enough to even be in this environment. The cello was uncased and Claire set it up sitting in the chair that was offered. She almost disappeared behind the big instrument. Kirk uncased his violin and prepared it, positioning himself to his sister's left.

Sergei was watching all of this and seemed to be amused but then asked if they knew his Trios Elegiaque number one. They blushed and indicated they didn't. He then asked if they could play Chopin's Piano Trio opus eight and they smiled, nodding their heads in a positive answer and looked relieved.

He played a few opening notes and they readied themselves by repeating them, then looked up and nodding that they were ready. Sergei led them into the score and twenty-five minutes went by with none in the room wanting to even breathe, as it was that good. Sergei stood and bowed to these two, very small, youngsters. He had played with a number of the best cellist and violinist in the world and these two were as good as many of those.

Everyone in the room knew how special it had been and the conversation was all about who they were, where had they studied before and with whom. Just then Kikolia Korsakov and his wife, Nadezhda, entered and all focused on them.

"What did I just hear from out in the hall. Play it again for me. Please!" was asked of the shocked youngsters. Sergei went to them and gave instructions that they would play it exactly as before. He asked if they knew Debussy Piano Trio in G major and they nodded yes one more time. "Just the first movement for an encore. Is that okay?" was answered with more nodding.

It went just as good the second time and the first movement of Debussy fit in nicely.

The invitation for returning the next evening was agreed upon and two more talented, young people would forever have a story of having entertained Rimsky-Korsakov at his request.

It had lasted longer than the usual gathering and after most of the guests had left the tiny Claire Munous asked Leokadiya if she could leave her cello overnight as it was getting late and they had a five block walk back to their apartment. It was of course fine with Leokadiya and she assured the young girl it would be safe. It was finally down to her, Cynthia, Sergei and Rose to do the clean up and start the planning for tomorrow.

Sergei walked Rose and Cynthia to their apartment and Rose quietly said to her daughter, "Say your goodnight here and be inside in a few minutes. Goodnight Sergei, it was a very nice evening for everyone there. You must take credit for this. You also have two young musicians that will tell their grandchildren of how they played a trio with the world famous pianist and composer, Sergei Rachmaninoff, in front of Rimsky-Korsakov." She smiled and closed the door behind her leaving her daughter to say goodnight to the man she would embrace and kiss with only the promise of what could be.

Chapter 28
1899-1900

Wednesday, the twenty-second, would be a very busy day and evening for those living in the apartment building that was home for Rimsky-Korsakov. The word about the gathering the night before had spread and Leokadiya knew what would happen that evening.

She had Stravinsky coming for his daily lesson, which always took more than the one hour it was supposed to last. She and Cynthia were planning a special presentation based on a song with no words, Cynthia playing the piano and she singing a single vowel soprano to the accompaniment. They had been toying around with this for several weeks and had composed the piano score with her matching it with her voice.

There was the seating to plan and they thought the Korsakovs, Cynthia's parents and Sergei's mother should have seating in chairs up front. Her piano and the space for the new members with their cello and violin would also need space. The expected two dozen attendees would have to stand. They had almost forgotten a spot for Sergei and had a good laugh after Cynthia had mentioned it.

The two of them, and Sergei, had brought up chairs from the Korsakov's apartment and placed them in position and thought there would be enough room for the rest standing behind them. Just then the youngsters, Claire and Kirk knocked on the open door and were welcomed in.

They handed Sergei a score that had Rachmaninoff Trio for piano, cello and violin on the top line.

The six there were treated to the practicing of Sergei's Elegiaque and it went so well it would be included in this evenings program. Another fun piece would be Leokadiya and Cynthia playing several of Sergei's short works for four hands. He would then play the second and third movements of his new concerto number 2. It would be a full program.

Sergei was planning to walk over to his mother's apartment early in the afternoon as the Beckmans had invited them both for a light dinner before the big event that night. He hadn't been able to ask her about coming for dinner, as the plans for attending the gathering had been made earlier. He thought he should give her some extra time to get ready.

She surprised him by accepting the dinner invitation with a sincerely meant, "How nice of them. Let me get ready and we can walk over."

In a few minutes Lyubov Rachmaninoff was ready, carrying a small bag with her shoes to replace her winter walking shoes when they got there. She would leave them in Fyodor's apartment, along with her overcoat, and they would make their entrance on time and respectably dressed. Sergei was thinking he couldn't remember the last time he had seen his mother happy, and looking so nice. Maybe what was happening in his life right now was exactly what they needed.

It was a good walk and they were early so they had taken their time. His mother pointed out the places she shopped for groceries, the other places she visited for her needs and they actually met several people she knew well enough to introduce her son.

Arriving at the Beckman's another friendly greeting with Samuel and Rose was a good start and the arrival of the Korsakov's was even better as they both recognized her and no introductions were necessary. First names were exchanged with some small talk. It was when Cynthia and Leokadiya came down from upstairs that a quick look of concern crossed Lyubov's face for the first time but was gone before the girls had noticed. Sergei had not missed it, however.

Dinner was excellent and the conversation was shared by all. Rose had made up plates for Claire and Kirk to take on their laps as there wasn't room at the table for them. They happily ate the unexpected dinner while listening to the conversation of the adults.

By 7:30 everyone from the apartment building were in place on the fifth floor. The music sheets needed were on the racks and the performers ready and relaxed. By 8:00 there was room for no more inside the apartment and several dozen, more were scattered about in the hallway standing, sitting and laying about on the floor.

Chapter 29
2022

The welcome home's had been taken care of and it was Cindy that started the conversation, "Well. what did you find out at Senar, or was it in Venice or Paris?"

They had rearranged their seating and formed a disorganized semi-circle. John was looking at Cindy as she asked her question and couldn't restrain a broad smile. "Cindy, you never disappoint. It is a nice trait and don't ever lose it. It is a beautiful love story that we found. I think I can put it that way, at least for now. I am going to have Robert and Sandra help us on the details and we will work on that later. What you need to know now is that what we talked about before did happen and we should be able to flush out the details with some research and with what is in the third box that Robert and Sandra are going through. This could be the genesis of their idea for a fictional book about Rachmaninoff."

Cindy was quivering with excitement and squeezing BJ's hand so hard that it hurt. He had covered her hand with his and then gently began massaging her arm seeking relief.

Wilma's eyes were dancing. "He was such a nice man. Whatever happened, I am sure he didn't hurt anyone. Tell us the story John. What happened? How did you find it out?" was Wilma's prodding.

John couldn't help himself. "I am going to tell you

the long story. Not a long, long story but I want to set it up so you can enjoy what happened that made it so special for Allison and me. Of course it happened in Venice."

BJ's phone chimed his incoming call theme, a short piano melody they all recognized, played by their favorite pianist. He looked up and said he had better take this one and left the room.

"Our young son seems to have grown up in the last few weeks," Ed saying this as he looked at Julia. "John, since you suggested BJ take over as Cindy's agent, I think he has found something he can partner with her. Totally different than the mathematics and physics he has been studying but he seems to be good at it. Good with people and numbers. I think it may work out very nicely for them both."

BJ was back and took his seat, apologized for the interruption but didn't elaborate on what the conversation had been about. A smile and nod to Cindy conveyed a un-spoken message and she smiled back. He turned toward John and asked, "What happened in Venice?"

"Venice is a better place than can be imagined and there were more people than it could accommodate. It was that way at all the major sights and you could hardly find space to stand. The lines for the major attractions were long and slow moving, which made for us the decision to just walk around and lose ourselves a fine choice. You can't get lost, you are on an island," was said by John in a manner that there was more to come before the magic they found in Venice would be shared with them.

He first described the flights and their arrival in Paris. He told Ben and Jennifer of the greeting from the attractive lady at the Champs du Mars Hotel who asked if they knew them as the Palm Desert address seemed familiar and she had checked back in her records finding your registration from 1994. "A nice couple and a nice story worth remembering." As John said this he could see Ben's face light up and Jennifer reaching for his hand. They both smiled when he told them of her comment pointing out the bakery on the corner down the street. Even more when he described their purchase of some cheese and a small bottle of wine on Rue Cler, the baguette at the bakery and finding the park bench with the view of the Effiel Tower.

It was then on to the visit to Senar. How beautiful it was there, the restoration of the Villa, it's decoration and displays and the manicured grounds. They were very impressed and had a good conference with the director. John was sure that they would like to have any or all of the Rachmaninoff documents but no offers, or suggestions of any, had been made by either side. All options were left open which he felt was the proper choice for the time being.

John leaned back in his chair and looked about the room. Each knew what was coming next as even John couldn't hide his own excitement in getting to tell the story that they all wanted to hear so badly.

Chapter 30
2022

"Venice! Where magic is around every corner. This time it was found in Campo San Maurizio, just a few blocks from our B & B. We had left Saint's Marks to others to escape the crowds and after a nice walk, crossing the Rialto Bridge twice and a rest after taking lunch at a small Trattoria, we wandered into the Campo. At one end was the Museo della Musica, a treasure chest of old musical instruments and secrets from one hundred and ten years ago."

John paused as he wanted to get said what needed to be said in the correct way. Cindy was his concern, but not to the degree it had been just two weeks earlier.

"First let me tell you about the museum. It is in an old church. A small cathedral. By this I mean the Church of San Maurizio that had been completely rebuilt and consecrated in 1580. It now houses a superb collection of the finest musical instruments from the last three centuries. The emphasis is of the classical Italian violins along with other related instruments of that period. As you walk into the cathedral, on the alter is a beautiful display of the finest of the collection, ready to be played. Through out are free standing display cabinets holding instruments, descriptions, sheet music, and notes that are at minimum, dazzling."

John took another pause, then continued, "It was in

the display of the restoration shop, with a large observa-
tion window, having work benches, tools, supplies, var-
nish and glue pots and even sawdust on the floor that my
story of this magic place comes into all of our lives."

He could see had the full attention until BJ made a
couple of clicks on his iPhone and on the big screen TV a
photo of the shop showed up in glorious color. It was over
John's shoulder and as he turned his first thought was that
was exactly the right thing to show his audience and his
second thought was why hadn't he thought of that. He
then asked BJ to show a few other views of the museum
and then return to the restoration area view.

"I should have thought of doing that BJ, as it
shows off the museum and you can imagine how Allison
and I felt when the director, as it turned out, gave us a personal tour. He asked if Allison played the piano and the
next thing we knew we were inside the restoration shop
and she was playing the two melodies of *1899 Cynthia* on
that big, long string piano you can see in the back of the
shop."

He then told what had happened next. That the director, Alberto Depolo, had invited them to his Wednesday
evening dinner party if Allison would play a few compositions for his guests on his grand piano. He described the
evening and how wonderful it was including the motor
boat ride on the Grand Canal to and from a dock near
their B & B.

"The next day, after trying to get lost in Venice a
second time and following a rest at the B & B, I suggested
a second visit to the museum. We were again greeted by
Alberto with the invitation to meet someone he thought
we would like to know. Gouvanni Santio was one of the

restoration experts and was just finishing a fine 1910 violin. He was placing and tightening the last string and making a last few additional adjustments. He asked Allison if she played, indicating the violin he was holding. I just stood there, watching the two of them as they talked about about the violin. He handed it to her and selected a bow that was on the bench. She did it again to me. She played a popular Italian folk song."

John offered Allison the chance to tell the rest of the story but she deferred to him as the better story teller.

"Gouvanni then told us he had a story to tell us. He had been at the dinner party, recognized Allison's playing of the Rachmaninoff pieces and when she played Cynthia's two melodies he said that he had heard them before and that he should tell them how that had happened. His grandfather, as a young man, was a favorite piano tuner for the Steinway Company and had been offered a position in New York in 1907."

Cindy excitedly interrupted John, "Sergei always had a piano turner travel with him on a long tour to tune each piano he was to play. Sometimes, if the piano was inferior, he would demand a Steinway Model D be brought in to replace it. In later years he owned four of them, scattered about the country and would call for one of his if he wasn't satisfied with what was provided. My great-grandmother told me all about that." She suddenly paused, then hesitantly asked if this was during the 1909-1910 American tour. "Oh my God John, could that mean what I think it might?"

Everyone in the room, except Wilma, immediately had seen the implication of what was about to be revealed. She then saw what was coming and her gasp turned their attention toward her as she blurted out, "He was married to Natalia and had two daughters by then. What was this Gouvanni's grandfather telling him."

"Cynthia Beckman was what he said to us. Just her name. He knew from our reactions that we knew about her and told us the rest of what his grandfather had told him just before he died. That he was part of the cover up of the affair between them during the time of Rachmaninoff's first American tour. Even that it had started before the first concert in North Hampton, Massachusetts in November, 1909. We also know that Cynthia Beckman bore a child, Anne Beckman, out of wedlock, in September, 1910."

John let this end the conversation for the time being but added, "Mike called me this morning and the estimate is that Cindy's piano and the rest of the contents from the storeroom in Wauseon should arrive here the day after tomorrow between twelve noon and five o'clock. The movers will reassemble the piano and position it at our direction. There are seven banker boxes, three book boxes, the piano bench and a bicycle. The last bringing a chuckle from the group.

All except for Cindy who was quietly sobbing in BJ's arms.

Chapter 31
1899-1900

Sergei stood off to one side and was lost in his thoughts. He had been watching Cynthia and Leokadiya as they managed things and could not help making the comparison with Natalia and her sister, Sophia. Natalia was the more attractive and by far the most competent in music. They were both good in organizational skills and good friends as well as being sisters. He could see that Cynthia and Leokadiya had developed somewhat the same relationship.

"Can I be in love with two women at the same time?" was a question that was crossing his mind and was one he had yet to answer. Natalia's revelation to him last week of her love for him had clarified something he had been unwilling to think about before. He liked her, was always comfortable when with her and found her attractive but it had never been this almost uncontrollable lust that he was feeling toward Cynthia. For some time he had been thinking it was time for him to marry, have a family and make a home for them and himself. It seemed almost ordained that he would marry Natalia and he did not reject that thought.

Someone had played some preparatory notes on the piano and he looked up to see Cynthia at the piano and Leokadiya standing next to it. All rational thoughts had left his mind as Leokadiya made her welcoming statements to the assembled group. He could only see the beauty of the woman he had just met a few days ago who he was helplessly in love with.

"We will start this evening's gathering with some music. Are you surprised? Just maybe you will be!" was Leokadiya's opening.

She then described how she would would sing two of Sergei's Six Songs Opus 8 number 2 and 5, Child, Thou Art As Beautiful As A Flower and The Dream. This would be followed by a song without words composed by Cynthia and sung again by her. They had been working on this for several months and hoped that it would be liked in how it was presented. The poetry came from Cynthia's melody, not from words of a poem.

Next would be the new stars in their midst, Kirk and Claire, who with Sergei at the piano would repeat their Chopin Piano Trio and then, with the aid of scoring on their music stand, they would perform his Trio Elegiaque Number 1 in G Minor.

Leokadiya then finished offering that if they still wanted more Sergei was willing to share his still unfinished first movement of his Concerto Number 2 for piano.

There was a buzz in the room and could also be heard coming from down the hallway. This was big time music in a very small space.

The three songs were done perfectly. Leokadiya's clear soprano voice was tempered by her for the small space as was Cynthia's piano playing. The obvious partnership that had been perfected by them made the songs seem effortlessly performed, with a love of music that could be shared. Cynthia's composition was a delight and was matched by Leokadiya's singing. It was a love song with no words and each there could place themselves in a romance only they could know.

Chopin was as played the night before although several thought it was even a better performance. It what came next that was the highlight of the evening and that was Sergei and the kids playing his Trio Elegiaque. He had composed this at age eighteen and this evening a direct comparison to Chopin's favorite Trio composition could be made. Rimsky-Korsakov didn't even wait to voice his opinion, "My God, it is better than Chopin's. I can't believe what I just heard."

It was time to take a break. Sergei was at a loss of what to do or say. Kirk and Claire were both in tears and were hugging him as best they could. They each were barely five foot tall and trying to hug the six foot three man was a bit awkward. Rimsky-Korsakov's words were still ringing in Sergei's ears and the look Cynthia was giving him was melting his heart.

There was some questions as to what to do next but soon the demand came from Sergei's mother, "Go ahead Sergei and play Number 2. The whole concerto. This is the right time, the right place and you have the talent it takes to play it. We should hear it now!"

It had been the right time and everyone there knew they had been treated to the music they would hear over and over for the rest of their lives.

Chapter 33
2022

As promised the piano moving van pulled up in front Ed and Julia's house at 2:00 pm on Friday, July eighth. Ed and BJ had emptied the living room of all the furniture and the straight hallway from from the front door, with only a one step rise, made for an easy move of the piano body on the dolly into the living room.

The piano was wrapped in two layers of moving blanket covers topped with plastic wrapping taped securely in place. The three legs, pedal arbor, fall board, music rack and lid were likewise wrapped. The piano bench was wrapped and boxed.

In addition were the storage boxes and the bicycle. Also, with some apologies from the movers, were a substantial pile of wood planks. They were the original shipping crate material for the piano used to ship it to Russia and back. They were of high quality, one inch black walnut. The shippers couldn't bear to put them in the dumpster at the Wauseon storage facility so included them in the delivery.

Once the two movers had all the piano packages in the living room they quickly removed the packing materials and re-assemble the Model C. Standing the piano case on the flat side the front and top legs were mounted, then with the piano rotated up the third leg placed. Then the pedal arbor, fall board, lid and music rack were positioned. The lid was opened, the prop placed and the bench located in the playing position.

It had taken less than three hours and Ed walked the movers back to their van. A thank you was given and to each a hundred dollar tip. Walking back inside the group had gathered. John, Allison, Wilma, Julia, BJ and Cindy had surrounded the piano and no one moved or said anything to Ed as he approached them. He looked toward Cindy and asked, "Do you want to see how far out of tune it is?"

She had a scared look on her face. It had been four years since she last played it and so much had happened in that time she couldn't hide the emotion overcoming her.

"Would you like me to go first?" Ed asked and then added, "Sit next to me and we will do it together." This was what was needed and the two sat together and adjusted the bench. Ed looked at Cindy. She returned the look and then spread her fingers and played the *1899 Cynthia* compositions. Both of them.

A smile came to her face and she nodded to Ed and he played the second movement of Concerto Number 2 for piano. When he finished Cindy reached for Ed and gave him a kiss on the cheek. "Thank you, thank all of you for giving me my life back. And finding my piano. It sounds good to me and a tuning will have it back to perfect. It is nice to have something perfect in your life."

The tuner, Ed and Julia's old friend Andy Lehto, was there the next morning and spent most of the day doing a complete tuning. Both Ed and Cindy went through several different Rachmaninoff compositions and after about an hour recital it was deemed by all that no piano had ever sounded better. Andy would come back on Monday and tune Ed's piano, which would be much easier as it had not sat four years in non-climate controlled storage unit in Ohio.

The three houses each now had a Steinway Model C piano in what had been the living rooms. The houses were almost identical in design but flipped. The breeze-way between Ben's and Ed and Julia's had their respective kitchens between them but the sounds from either piano carried clearly through the space. Cindy would now do almost all her practicing on her piano and Ed would use his in Ben's house. A second digital keyboard was purchased and both would occasionally use one with headphones which gave some relief for those caught between the two pianists.

Cindy was ready for Rachmaninoff Number 5 and was starting the learning curve on Number 6. The early September dates for the concerts was being planned and they hoped to do both in that month.

At John and Allison's place there was a fair amount of violin being heard, some of which was quite nice. Ed, or Cindy, would sometimes play pieces for piano and violin and that was also becoming a good break for everyone. John had his office and was busy with his researcher putting the pieces together of Cindy's ancestral link to Sergei Rachmaninoff.

It would be in the contents of one of the boxes of from Ohio that would cause excitement for the group. Robert and Sandra having returned, made the discovery enjoyed by the entire team together.

Chapter 34
2022

Cindy and BJ had arranged a six foot folding leg table with two chairs in their bedroom and the boxes from Ohio were stacked along the wall. The table was covered with a cloth blanket and they began the inspection of the contents. The bicycle and the boards were in the garage. The contents of the rental storage in Wauseon, Ohio were now all in one place in Palm Desert, California.

The first box they set on the table was one of the three book boxes and it was no surprise that it contained books. Very old books, mostly with titles not recognized, all neatly inscribed with the owners name and dated. BJ entered one with title and author into the Abe Books website. "Wow, look at this!" he said as he showed the $400 asking price to Cindy. A second book showed a lesser, but still a respectable amount.

They carefully placed all the books on the table and could see they were in very good condition, belonged to a Elizabeth Proxmire and were dated from 1850 to 1900. The publishing dates were earlier indicating the hand written dates were when she became the owner. The other two book boxes held mostly the same type of books in the same condition. This apparently was the library of Elizabeth Proxmire and they had no idea who she was.

It was BJ that noticed in the second box several books that had a different look and decided to pull out a particularly bedraggled one, with a red cover. Goops And How To Be Them. He opened it up and inscribed on the cover page was "For Rose Anne Beckman on her birthday, September 17, 1910. From your mother who will always love you."

"Look at this, Cindy. This is different. Not like the others. It is a children's book and has been read a lot. Almost worn out."

Cindy took the book from BJ and held it for several minutes, then opened it to the first page reading the inscription. She slowly spoke with tears forming and sliding down her cheeks. "G G Anne read me these stories, over and over again. 'The Goops they lick their fingers and the Goops they lick their knives; They spill their broth on the tablecloths . . . .'," then letting her voice fade away. She suddenly continued, "It was she who told me the stories of being with Rachmaninoff, loving him and being loved by him. Of writing music with him. I can remember being held in her lap, as she rocked back and forth, telling me those stories but it was her mother that had been there. It was her mother, Cynthia Beckman, that had been with him. I just let those stories become mine as I learned to play and love his music. It all makes sense to me now, BJ. It had to be something like that."

Cindy stood up and clutched the book to her breast and took BJ's hand. "We have to tell John about this. He already knows, I am sure, but he needs to know I know now. The pieces of the puzzle are coming together and making sense. We need to find out what happened between Cynthia Beckman and Rachmaninoff that has me now standing here next to you."

As they walked from their bedroom Cindy stopped

when she saw her piano. The lid had been left up and the sunshine from outside was reflecting off the golden frame and strings. She stopped, went to it and sat on the bench. Setting aside the book next to her she started to play the *1899 Cynthia* scores and then the short passage of the one that had Rachmaninoff's writing of "can a man love two women at the same time" message on the top of the partial music sheet.

She played it twice and then looked up at BJ and asked, "This was written by Cynthia Beckman and it was a love letter to him. I wonder what she wrote on the bottom of the page that had him tear it off. He kept the music and his question but didn't want anyone to know about what she might have written."

Ed had been outside with the rest of the group enjoying an after breakfast period of conversation when he heard Cindy playing her special pieces. The sound was muted from the distance and walls but had filtered through the breezeway and out the open patio doors of Ben's house. He went inside to join them but stopped in the kitchen area, silently listening to Cindy playing and heard what she said to BJ.

He moved forward and when he saw Cindy and his son together, pondering her questions and what it must mean, a feeling of confidence for the two of them came over him. He was now sure they had a relationship very much like he and Julia had and that their lives together would as good as theirs has been.

Chapter 35
1899-1900

The Wednesday gathering had been a resounding success. It was more a recital with some of the best music those attending had ever heard. After most had left and Sergei had helped Cynthia's father carry the extra chairs back to Rimsky-Korsakov's, he walked his mother back to her apartment. He was tired and decided to spend the night there.

It wasn't until they were almost to the apartment that she brought up Natalia's name into the conversation. When comfortably inside, and with cups of coffee in hand, she said what was on her mind and it was what Sergei was anticipating.

"We all expect you will be choosing Natalia to be your wife. You know she is in love with you. She always has been. She has watched you make a fool of yourself with little Vera Skalon, heard some stories about a married gypsy woman teasing you and cannot wait too much longer for your consideration. And now this Cynthia Beckman shows up. She will be back in America in a month, or less, and I have no doubt that her father will never let his only daughter stay here in Russia with an aspiring musician."

It was a long speech for Lyubov to make and she slumped into her favorite chair with an audible grunt. Sergei also sat down and looked at his mother. Once he failed his academic classes at the Saint Petersburg Conservatory and was sent to the Conservatory in Moscow she had given up her involvement in his day to day life. She had sent her twelve year old boy to an unfamiliar place but fortunately had her sister and her family there to provide some sense of home he needed.

"I know you are right. I truly like Natalia and until a week ago was thinking she would be the right one for me. It was time and I had made the decision to ask her to marry me. I have no way to describe what has just happened with Cynthia Beckman. Also, I am sure after she goes back to America I will never see her again. My heart feels like it is broken right now.

"Don't laugh at me. Such things shouldn't happen like this," Sergei said this as if making a confession, but then added, "She, her parents and Leokadiya have given me my life back. I will go back to Moscow, visit Tolstoy again and do with Dr. Dahl whatever it is I am supposed to but this is my secret, I feel ready to do what you are all are expecting of me and I am now sure I can do it. This is my secret and I want you to keep it that way for me. I will ask Natalia to marry me when I return to Moscow and I will have no regrets about doing so."

Cynthia and Leokadiya had finished cleaning up the apartment, and the hallway, as the students had left a mess. Claire and Kirk had helped a little and then left for their long walk back to their apartment struggling with the large cello in it's case.

The girls took a seat in the best chairs in the parlor and each had a glass of wine in hand. Looking at each other they started to laugh. In the three years a friendship had been established between them that was closer than most sisters have. There were no secrets between them and no subjects were left unspoken between them.

The laughter was that both knew the other was in love with Sergei Rachmaninoff. The man and his music, and it had all happened in the last few days starting with the train trip from Moscow to Saint Petersburg.

Cynthia was first, telling Leokadiya of what she had told Sergei that first night when she walked him to Fyodor's apartment door. That she loved him and wanted to make love to him.

"It didn't scare him, or embarrass him. We kissed and that was all that happened. But I meant it then and I still mean it. I don't think there is any way we will be together before I leave for home in America. He goes back to Moscow the first week of January and I am not sure when we have to leave as father is making the arrangements now." Cynthia said this calmly but Leokadiya could sense her sadness.

"I have the same feelings for him. I have seen him several times, heard him play and know some of his history. He is nothing like what I had expected. He has a sense of humor, is friendly, polite and really is a nice person. None of that was what I was prepared for from the gossip here in Saint Petersburg. Did you see the way he treated the two students? How he helped them be even better than they had been even a few minutes before they met him. He brings out the best in others and that is something I would like to have close to me. "

Leokadiya leaned back and took another swallow of wine, nearly emptying her glass. Nodding toward Cynthia she stood, retrieved the bottle and filled their glasses.

"He had a tough childhood in a way considering

his first years. His father lost all his mother's dowry and they ended up crowded into the small apartment she is still living in. At one time they had five estates, several of which were very nice. His talent was discovered early and he was enrolled in the Conservatory here at age ten. He didn't do his homework and was pushed out and sent to the Moscow Conservatory two years later, a very lonely and sad young boy. He was placed into a top class run by an odd teacher, Nikolai Zverev. He took only three students, all boys, and they lived in his house. There were three pianos in the same room and one was dedicated for teaching. Each boy had a two hour lesson each day, six days a week. On Sunday was an open house and the various luminaries of the music world would drop in to hear the students perform and comment on their progress. It must have been chaos when the constant practicing was done together."

They both made a toast to their love of Sergei and it wasn't long until the glasses needed to be refilled. The talk then evolved to their own experiences with men and it turned out there hadn't been many. Actually none. That caused the bottle to be emptied and then Cynthia headed for her apartment. Her parents greeted her pleasantly and allowed her to go to her bedroom without much comment other than it had been a fabulous evening and they were proud of her.

Chapter 36
1899-1900

Sergei had breakfast with his mother and with her promise to keep his recovery from depression between them was given the first real hug he could remember in years.

He was back in Fyodor's apartment by ten o'clock cold, lonely and confused. For all intensive purposes he was now engaged to be married to Natalia and in the apartment below was someone he thought he was in love with. "How could his life have gotten so complex when he had just come out from under a dismal cloud of depression and the doubt he had been fighting for almost three years," were the thoughts running through his mind.

He sat down in front of Fyodor's upright piano and started playing a combination of familiar chords and melodies. He wasn't paying any attention to what he was doing as his thoughts of Cynthia were dominate in his mind. He could visualize them together, walking in fields of grain as it was in his summers at Ivanovka where life was simpler. He could imaging making love to her there not thinking of anything but to make her happy.

Slowly the sounds of the piano penetrated his consciousness and he began to hear what he was playing. It was good and his years of repeating certain portions of what he liked forced him to put all else out of his mind. He grabbed some music sheets and a pencil and quickly noted a few bars, played them and then continued. Two hours later he had five sheets of music scribbled out and he stopped.

Looking around the room he realized where he was and what he had been doing. He read the music and then played through it. A few more changes and then he played through it again.

A smile came to his face and he was suddenly hungry. He decided it was time to clean up and see if his new muse was at home. "At least for the next few days he could be in love with two women at the same time. One would be gone in a few days and the other would be with him the rest of his life," was his thought as he changed clothes and tending to making himself more presentable.

He knocked on the Beckman's apartment and there was no answer. A second knock and it appeared no one was there. He went up to the fifth floor and repeated his knocking on Leokadiya's door with the same results.

As he sat in one of the chairs in Fyodor's apartment a sadness enveloped him and his spirits descended into melancholy. He didn't want to feel this way. Just a few hours ago he was coming back to life and settling into which direction his future should go. He had even composed a nice little piece of music with out any effort. It had come so easily he was ready to expand on it into something major. Now he didn't want to hear it again.

There was a knock on the door and when he opened it all the sadness left him and the kiss he received from Cynthia Beckman had his world intact again.

A early dinner was being planed and he was invited. "Would he like to join them?" Cynthia asked but she hadn't pushed away from him yet. She was searching his eyes and let his hands pull her closer against him. "We are expected now and it is going to have to be this way." He stood back, just in time from not providing a further embarrassment to himself.

"I have something I want you to play. I will get it and we can get you back in time to not worry your mother and father."

Sergei stepped back into the apartment and picked up the five sheets off the music rack, returned to Cynthia and in a few minutes he was being welcomed into the Beckman's apartment that was now brightly decorated for the American Christmas, on the Julian calendar date of December 25, just four days away.

Chapter 37
2022

In Palm Desert the group was all together in the three houses and working again as a team. The main effort for Ed, Cindy and BJ was preparing for the performance of Rachmaninoff Number 5. The dates were September 22 and 24. Thursday evening's premier and a Saturday matinee and evening repeat performances. Number 6 was scheduled for October 13 and 15 with the same format of Thursday premier and Saturday the two performances.

Much to everyone's surprise, including himself, BJ's acting as manager for these events was going smoothly. He was enjoying what he was doing and was good at it. John had turned over all the responsibilities to him and just peeked in occasionally to ask how things were going. The staff at the McCallum Theater were more than satisfied and the orchestra members were delighted with what had come their way.

Julia, with help from Jennifer, had taken charge of all things domestic. Each morning breakfast was organized in Ben and Jennifer's kitchen and generally taken out poolside. Wilma was in heaven and every morning had a sparkle in her eyes that all could enjoy. To see an elderly woman so happy and excited with each day's beginning was making theirs even better.

John and Allison had recovered from their trip to Europe and were concentrating the trail of Cindy's ancestry. Robert and Sandra were modifying the story they were writing on Rachmaninoff, the fictional interpretation, as the discoveries were being made.

It was what happened next that put everyone focused on the unveiling of the main story of Cindy's infatuation of having been with Rachmaninoff. In the bottom of one of the bankers boxes there was a slender, old and worn letter sized box. Cindy had been going through the boxes from the storage room and this was one of the last two. She had found nothing of real interest until she saw the small box and carefully lifted it out and placing it on the table.

It had been a long day already and she was ready to turn in for the night. BJ was in bed, looking like he was just about to fall asleep. She had the urge to climb in next to him and let sleep come for her unless he wanted to stay awake a little longer.

But first she carefully lifted the top off the box and set it aside. Exposed was a letter, hand written and in Russian. She couldn't read it but it was clearly written and the handwriting was familiar to her. It was the same as the writing by Rachmaninoff on the top of the partial sheet of music she had often played. She knew immediately who it had been written to and who had written it. The paper looked very fragile and there were several round stains scattered about on it's surface. At the bottom, written in English was, "I love you. Seryozha." Cindy knew that Seryozha was Sergei's name when being used with affection.

Cindy smiled as she realized the box contained love letters from Sergei Rachmaninoff to her great-great-grandmother, Cynthia Beckman. These letters would answer the questions of the affair between the two of them that had resulted in her being here. Of being alive. Being born.

She carefully placed the top back on the box and left it on the table. Tomorrow morning the group would have a new project and all would participate. Deciphering this love story would find all of them on another adventure of a lifetime. How much more fun could life be than right now for this group of friends.

Cindy looked at BJ before turning off the desk lamp. He was handsome, just like his father. His father's half Vietnamese heredity was only discernible in his eyes and skin color and tone. BJ's was very similar and she liked the look and feel of his skin. BJ was also a kind human being and she loved that even more.

Turning off the light she slipped into bed and positioned herself on her side facing him. She felt his hand on her shoulder and enjoyed how he slid it down over her side to her waist, then up on the curve of her hip. He didn't wake, left his hand in place for a few minutes then brought it back to himself. She moved slightly to get comfortable and her sleep came quickly.

Chapter 38
2022

Cindy and BJ were, as usual, the last one's up for breakfast and arrived sleepy eyed, bare foot and dressed in shorts and T-shirts. Good mornings were exchanged and it was Wilma who asked it first, "What are you hiding from us this morning? Come on now, tell us!"

They looked at each other and Cindy answered, "I found a small box of love letters from Sergei to Cynthia Beckman. There must be at least twenty. They are old and look fragile so I only looked at the one on top. They are hand written in Russian and it is in the same handwriting that Sergei wrote the can I love two women at the same time note."

John had sat up so suddenly he almost sent his empty plate into the pool. Allison clapped her hands together and shouted "Oh Boy, Oh Boy!" Even Ben, who usually sat quietly in his favorite chair in the shade, let out an heart felt, "Hurrah!"

They all knew what this meant. It would be his responses to Cynthia Beckman's letters to him. They could interpret what she had written by his responses and it should clearly demonstrate how the affair that must have occurred matured.

Robert and Sandra realized what it would mean for them as much of the previous interpretations of Rachmaninoff's life was from the letters he wrote to others.

This would be as important, in some ways, as the discovery of the music itself. They, again, now had something no one had known existed.

John gathered his thoughts and quickly started the organization of the morning's efforts. Julia could set up the copy system digitizing each letter. They would follow the curator techniques they had used on the sheet music. He would then forward the digital copies to his translator and they would soon know some important details on how their story would end.

Two hours later twenty-seven letters, comprised of a total of forty-two pages, had been digitized. At 4:30 pm that afternoon the first letter translation was on their computers and iPads. The letter was dated 17 February 1900.

Dear Cynthia Beckman,

How I miss you. Your smile, your energy, just your being in my life for that short time.

I am doing what I am supposed to do and telling no one about you. And my own secret is safe.

Fyodor went with me to see Tolstoy and it was a disaster. I went thinking he was a God and left thinking he was just an angry old man.

Dr. Dahl is doctoring me. I think he knows I have already recovered from my depression. That I am trying to fool him so as to have good conversation and have someone to tell me how fine I am. Maybe it is he who needs the these sessions.

The arrangements to have Leokadiya receive my mail from you, assuming there will be some, will work out fine. I will secretively read it alone in my little bedroom here at the Satin's. Please write me if you haven't already. If you have already, write another and send it to me.

Natalia treats me the same and I grow fonder of her presence, as I must do. I think everyone here is only waiting for the date to be set for our marriage. It won't be soon as both the church and the bureaucrats are opposed to it. Her mother, Varvara Satina, is managing the event so it will happen. None can say no to her more than once.

I am at peace with this. It will work out for the best.

I was out in public this evening for the first time this year. Musician and conductor at the Large Hall of the Nobility. We started with Beethoven's Egmont Overture which went well. I like it and so does the small orchestra I conducted. Several arias with my accompanying the singers. A Rubinstein two piano piece with Alexander Goldenweiser on the second piano and a finale with Fyodor singing the best parts of Aleko. What a great voice. He makes any event worth attending.

Why can't you be here to share in my humble life?
Before you fall asleep tonight, kiss me once more.
I love you.
Seryozha

They were all reading it at the same time on their own devices. John had printed several copies, giving one to Wilma, Ben and keeping one for himself. All was quiet. It was Wilma who finally said it, and said it best. "Why is being in love sometimes so painful."

Cindy and BJ were standing close together. He was watching the others and as if choreographed the couples moved toward each other, his mother kissing his father with a tender kiss and then with a smile taking his hand in hers. Sandra had done the same with Robert and Jennifer moved closer to Ben on the chaise lounge and gave him a hug and a kiss on the forehead. Wilma observed it all and tears were showing on her cheeks.

"What's going on?" was BJ's question as Cindy was squeezing his hand even tighter. She said in a voice he hadn't heard before, "You will discover it when the time is right, and it had better be with me." She gave him a kiss and continued, "You don't need to find out the why, yet."

BJ took a second look at Cindy and thought he had an inkling as his love for her almost overwhelmed him.

Chapter 39
1899-1900

To Sergei's eyes the apartment sparkled. Outside the sun had come out from behind a gray mist, the curtains had been opened and the light, clear and bright, filled the room. There was a branch of needled pine boughs on the table decorated as a Christmas tree might be and his spirits were lifted. One more look in Cynthia's direction had him happy and weak in the knees again.

Leokadiya saved him from saying anything foolish on how he felt at that moment by asking him about the music sheets he was holding in his hand. He said his hello's to Rose and Samuel and a nod of thank you to Leokadiya was made, which she understood and accepted with a smile.

"It is a short composition I put together this morning that I think has some prospects. I have only played it through once." Sergei found his breath a bit short and hoped he didn't look the way he was feeling.

Cynthia didn't wait and asked, "Let us see it!" looking at Leokadiya, and not noticing her parents smile at their daughter not letting another get between herself and Sergei.

He handed the sheets to Cynthia and the two went to the piano, sat on the bench together and the score was placed on the music rack. They read the score on the first page, went to the next and then on to the last of the five.

Leokadiya, not to be out done, said, "I get to play it first, then Cynthia can try to out do me and then the composer can see if he can do any better." She arranged herself with a little nudge to Cynthia to move over and the music began.

When she finished there was a silence that lasted long enough to worry Sergei for just a minute, but then he started to relax as he knew how good it was.

"I won't try to out do that. Sergei, it is wonderful. You can expand on it to as big a piece as you want. It's increditable." Cynthia was having trouble expressing herself and no on else wanted to break the spell.

It was Sergei's turn and he did out do Leokadiya's playing. He added some more melodies to the whole as they came to his mind.

They would find their place to paper later. It had been a very good start to the afternoon and the early dinner added to this. He had found a new family and was beginning to think he belonged.

The conversation was lively and carried on by all. Even Rose, who seemed to Sergei to be somewhat reserved, shared with several stories about her daughter that brought him even more into this American family.

His goodnight to Cynthia that night was as the night before and the parting was the same painful experience for him. She touched his lips with her finger tips after the long kiss and told him he was now a part of not only her life but of her mother and father's. That their relationship, for now, would have to remain as it was.

"Someday we will be together as we want it to be right now. I will make sure it happens. I promise you that," she told him as she turned away and left him standing in the hallway.

A few minutes later Sergei was in Fyodor's apartment looking out the window in the darkening evening. On the street he could see a young couple walking under a street lamp, the light snow sparkling as it slowly fell dusting their hats and coats. They stopped and kissed, then laughing, ran quickly into the doorway of the building across the way. Sergei was wishing that it was he and Cynthia and his tear's began to fall.

Chapter 40
1899-1900

Christmas day, at least the date of December 25 on the Julian calendar used in Russia, was now here and Sergei couldn't decide on whether he was happy or sad. Christmas in Russia, celebrated thirteen days from now, was January 7 of the new year and would be the last good day before he felt he must start worrying about what the new year would bring.

The last decade had seemed to only bring sorrow into his life. Good things had happened but many truly bad things had occurred that left him weak in mind and heart. This last week had made an dramatic change for him. He woke up this American Christmas morning with something to look forward to. To spend time with Cynthia and her family. Leokadiya would be there and Nicolai Rimsky-Korsakov and his wife would also be guests at dinner. Even his mother would be with them and she was looking forward to it with genuine enthusiasm.

He hadn't dressed yet and was at Fyodor's piano composing, at will, one melody after another. Just thinking of one good thing about this week would have another short score on paper. Just little pieces that begged for more to be done but then it was off to another thought and another few bars of something else. It was fun and he was enjoying what was happening.

The morning hadn't started out this way as he had

woken up reflecting on the dark periods of his childhood years. The death of his little sister, Sophia, in 1883 and his father abandoning the family a few months later. Five years later his older sister, Yelena, who was the musical talent in the family that he had looked up to, died breaking all of their hearts, especially his mother's.

His thoughts were then on the passing of two important adults in his life. Nikolai Zverev, his teacher and who he had lived with for three years at the Moscow Conservator, had died in September of 1893. Then a month later Tchaikovsky, whose brief friendship and advice had meant so much to him. His Trio Elegiance was composed in his memory. Sergei was now beginning to think in terms of his own possible death which was not helpful for someone so young.

After he had graduated from the Moscow Conservatory he was expected to earn his own living with his talents. He had secured numerous positions that took much time but with only small financial rewards. He was now twenty-six and still adrift. Then Cynthia Beckman appeared as if in a dream. He feared he would wake up and be sitting next to the over weight man in economy on the train to Saint Petersburg. He could almost smell the garlic and sausage contained in the oily paper bag the fat man had been holding in his lap.

The knock on the door cleared his mind of these thoughts and he opened the door before he remembered he hadn't yet dressed that morning. He was standing in front of Cynthia in his under shorts and wrinkled shirt.

"Hi good looking. You look quite nice this morning, dressed so appropriately to escort me to breakfast with my parents." Her laughter at first caused an embarrassed look come over his face but that disappeared as she reached for him and kissed him. "Someday I will greet the new day with you, better dressed, or not dressed at all, and it will be more than breakfast with my parents on a Christmas morning. But for now you better get it together and be at our apartment in fifteen minutes." She started to turn away, came back into his arms and they held each other for a few moments more. "Someday, someplace it will happen for us. I promise you, mister Sergei Rachmaninoff."

The next minute Sergei stood in the doorway and watched her go to the stairwell and disappear from sight. Ten minutes later he was knocking on her door and she greeted him with a quick kiss and he entered a life the likes of which he had never known before.

Samuel was at the cook stove removing some long strips of bacon from a big skillet. He laid them out on paper and poured the fat from the skillet in a metal cup. Ladling batter into the skillet in equal amounts, four pancakes were formed. A minute later turned over, another minute, then four perfect pancakes were placed in a tin box to keep warm A spoonful of bacon fat was added to the skillet and soon four more pancakes were stored.

Places were set for the four of them and breakfast was served. Sergei offered that they were the best pancakes he had every eaten and he had tried both a maple syrup and a honey topping. Coffee was taken and the mood was relaxed and the conversation comfortable.

It was after the ladies had tended the dirty dishes and put things away that Samuel asked Sergei, casually, if he could make a good living from his music.

Surprising all three Beckmans, he described the

facets of the three areas he was pursuing, performance, composition and conducting including what was expected in rubles. The amounts could vary a great deal. He gave some details of his first successful piece, the opera Aleko. He could expect payments when it was performed and could also take the role as the conductor and be paid separately for that. As for compositions, it was similar in that he could be paid by the publishing house, both initially and then per copy sold. Also if it was performed by others. Again he could conduct or perform his own work and be paid on that basis.

Samuel asked if he had a management team in place. Sergei looked puzzled by this and Samuel added, "Some times you need more than one person helping you, specialist are most helpful. You might seek out opinions from others that are making it into the big earners category. What they have learned. The business world can often be cruel to the innocent."

The conversation returned to less demanding subjects and Sergei begged his leave to walk over to his mother's as he was expected for a light lunch. They would walk back before it got dark.

Chapter 41
2022

It was decided by John that they should do no more with the letters until the translations were all in hand. The first letter indicated that Cynthia Beckman had returned to America with her parents and Rachmaninoff was attempting to further a lasting friendship that may find her promises to him fulfilled.

The birth of her only child had occurred about eight months after Rachmaninoff's American tour had finished. It was too much of a coincidence to not to have been then when they would consummate their love for each other, some nine years later. Only from these secret letters over those years would they learn how it happened. The twenty-seven letters should also hold a trove of information about Rachmaninoff over that period.

Sandra and Robert had been concentrating on the life of Rachmaninoff with the printed literature published and the many encyclopedia type compilations available on-line. No where were the Beckmans mentioned, nor any implications of what had happened in Rachmaninoff's life over the final days of 1899 through the first days of 1900.

Their searches would now be concentrated on that period, on the information around the dates of the letters and then on the later dates that spanned a period from November 4, 1909 through January 31, 1910, which book-ends his American tour.

Cynthia's Dreams

John, with help from his researcher, was getting most of the details lined up in the lineage from Cynthia Beckman to their Cynthia Anne Ashbaugh. There were a few blanks but that shouldn't be a problem and provided them time to work along some of the lines Robert and Sandra were following.

Ed and Julia were more than willing to have the others figure it all out. Their main concern was for BJ but he seemed to really enjoy working with the movers and shakers of the classical music world and so far everything he involved himself was turning out the better because of his efforts. Cindy seemed to be at peace and totally comfortable with playing at the highest level in classical piano. Ed was amazed at her confidence. He had six performances scheduled as the featured pianist and he needed some time away from all the hubbub in the search for her past.

Ben, Jennifer and Wilma watched what needed to be watched and they thought they were doing a good job doing this. Occasionally they would catch something that would be of help, but they concentrated just on the watching.

Cynthia Anne Ashbaugh's lineage was an easy task for John's researcher and posed no real problems in discovery. Great-grandmother Rose Anne Beckman was the daughter of Cynthia Beckman, born out of wedlock and the father was never identified. She had married George Albert Whyte and they had three children, two boys and a daughter. The daughter, Elizabeth Rose Whyte, had married Alexander Paul Mason and it was their daughter, Shirley Catherine Mason that would come to Wauseon, Ohio and marry Ash Ashbaugh who were Cindy's parents.

Nothing in the knowledge of this ancestry would have predicted the talent that had brought all of them working on this project together.

Two days later they had all twenty-seven letters translated. Each had been read and a multitude of possibilities detected. Robert and Sandra had re-arranged their collection of receipts, notes and memorabilia in that time frame. The years around 1909 and 1910 showed a population of these small items relative to the years on either side. Sandra was first to see the very small letters of *"cb"* on a number receipts, especially hotels and restaurants. Also, there were a number where the concert dates had a few days free between them. They had something to work with that now made sense.

John and Allison were concentrating on the letters. Each of the group had paper copies and each enjoyed the personal writing's of Rachmaninoff. From the romance, his highs and lows, humor, to plans and accomplishments. Each had their own reaction to what they were privileged to read. For John, it was putting together the pieces of the story into a complete one. He was in his element.

John mused, "The RMS Lucania of the Cunard Line had been making trans-Atlantic crossings from Liverpool, England since 1894 but at best a letter like the 17 February, 1900 one would have taken at least two to three weeks to get from Moscow, or Saint Petersburg, to Cleveland, Ohio. Maybe even longer and to receive a response would mean a month, or more, between letters." Rachmaninoff's request for Cynthia to write even if she hadn't received a response could be understood.

They did have one other piece of information that would help in the timing of what they were looking for.

Rachmaninoff had a suite at the Netherland Hotel on Fifth Avenue during his American Tour.

John called his researcher and had a very short conversation. "Mike, can you find out if Cynthia Beckman reserved a room at the Netherland Hotel on Fifth Avenue, New York City, around the same time. Maybe the first week of November, 1909?"

The call was returned thirty minutes later and on the speaker phone Mike answered, "Yes, there was a reservation for Cynthia Beckman and the room was occupied."

John looked at Allison and the smile she gave him told him many things, all of them good.

Mike then added the proverbial one more thing, "Both Rachmaninoff's room and Cynthia's were reserved for the duration of Rachmaninoff's stay in America and on the same floor," and then he added, "Her reservation was from October 25, 1909 to February 4, 1910."

The letters were now the keys. Twenty-seven over a period of approximately ten years. They were spaced out with five written before the important date of 29 April, 1902, Rachmaninoff's marriage to Natalia Satina. He had earlier wrote to the Skalon sisters, addressed to Natalia Skalon, "At the end of this month I shall have the carelessness to get married." He ended the letter, "Goodbye, Tatusha! To sum up this letter: forgive me, send me a gift and feel sorry for me."

This would be the last letter sent to, or one responded to, to the Skalon sisters, They were always addressed to the oldest, Natalia, but the contents were meant for Vera, the youngest of the three. She had been Rachmaninoff's first love, them meeting when he was seventeen and she fifteen. Her mother had forbid any direct contact between them after she caught them holding hands. The sisters had teased him for years. Vera became engaged, and then married, with them not telling him by the time he told them of his betrothal to Natalia Satina.

The letters to Cynthia Beckman would be different. They had both thought that their love would never be consummated as the Beckman's would go back to America and Sergei had no idea at that time where his music would take him. The letters were the story of unrequited love that they could carry on with until it had no meaning for one or the other, or either. It would end in a different way, however, but it started with that first letter Rachmaninoff wrote responding to Cynthia's first letter to him.

Chapter 42
1899-1900

Sergei enjoyed the walk to his mother's apartment. The hubbub of Christmas planning at the Beckman's was a bit much and it had been a long time since Christmas had any real meaning for him. Most of his close family relationships had been nurtured during the summer months spent at the Satin's estate, Ivanovka, near Tambov and Nizhny Novgorod, about 260 miles southwest of Moscow. It was here he had met Vera Skalon, his childhood sweetheart, became close to his mother's sister's family, the Satins, and his now probable wife to be, his first cousin Natalia.

As he leisurely wandered along the familiar route he was thinking of the girls and women in his life. At twenty-six he had had few real sexual experiences in his life. With Vera Skalon it was just holding hands and an occasional kiss, which had to be stolen when the occasion permitted. He had no doubt she told everything they did to her older sisters, to their joint amusement, about his awkwardness.

It was different with Anna, the exotic gypsy wife of Pyotr Lodyzhensky, a concert master cellist and composer with whom he had become friends. She was different in every way from the silly Vera. A married woman in her mid-thirties, unashamedly flirtatious, with red painted lips and dark flashing eyes. For over a month he had been their guest every evening and when Pyotr would tire playing his marvelous cello repertoire with his piano accompaniment, she would continue her dancing, swaying about the room and then concentrate on bedeviling him with the suggestion of what was available if only they could be alone. They never were alone but the gypsy life she represented became a central theme in much of his compositions for sometime.

Sergei smiled at these thoughts of Vera and Anna and then the present one to think about, Cynthia Beckman. She had left no doubt about what she wanted with him if it had only been possible. He knew it would be good with her and he had never had that confident feeling with another woman. He also felt certain he would never find out what it would be like.

Arriving at his destination he put all these thoughts aside and knocked on his mother's apartment door. She seemed to be happy, dressed nicely and ready for the walk back to the Beckmans. But first she asked him if he had a gift for Cynthia. She was not surprised that he hadn't one.

"I was not much of a mother for you Sergei. When I needed to be one the most, our family had fallen apart. My most talented child was sent off to the Conservatory to be raised by others. You need a gift for Cynthia even though she will be leaving your life in a few days. You're in love with her and that's okay if you realize that it is Natalia that is the one to marry and make your life with. Your fondness for her will grow into love and it will be a good life and marriage. Still, you owe a gift to Cynthia for what she has done to help you escape from your problems. I have something you can give her."

She put her satchel down and went back into the

apartment. Finding a small box on the shelf in the closet she brought it out and motioned for Sergei to sit next to her on the couch.

Removing the lid she rummaged around among a number of small trinkets, boxes and small leather bags with draw strings. She took one of these small bags out and handed it to him. He pulled open the top of the bag and emptied the contents in his had. It was a locket style fob on a gold chain. Almost a cylinder in shape, like a small bottle, but very delicately engraved and filigreed in gold and colors. The proportions were just right to wear as a woman's pendant.

He held up it to the light and let it slowly rotate. He was fascinated by how such a small item could be so beautiful. "What is it? It is really nice and she will love it. I like it and I want to see her wearing it." Sergei was moved and handing it it back to his mother and she held it up to the light just as he had.

"This has a story that I will tell you before we wrap it up. Your father bought this just after you were born and brought it home to me as a present." She had said this softly as she grasped the top, gently twisting the lower portion. Two turns had them separated and she turned the cylinder upside down. A small papered packet slid into her palm.

Sergei could see the emotion on her face and the moister forming in her eyes. Carefully opening the packet a tiny woven braid of fine blond hair was exposed.

"This was cut from the shock of hair you had when you were born and at a time when my life was so much better than you have ever known. I think it is your Cynthia that should have this."

Chapter 43
1899-1900

It was a very pleasant walk from the apartment to the Beckman's. Sergei had no memory of his mother ever showing the happiness she was now exhibiting. She had threaded her arm through his and he clasped her hand resting on his arm.

While they had been inside a short snow shower had passed through, an inch of pure white snow covered over all the discolored snow and a few remaining flakes were sparkling in the lights. It was 4:30 pm as they reached the apartment building on Zagorodny Prospekt and neither wanted to go inside.

They did and the sights from outside were easily replaced by those inside. Rose, Cynthia and Leokadiya were squeezed into the kitchen and the chatter and activity was non-stop. Nikolia and Nadezhda Korsakov were seated on the love seat and they invited Sergei's mother to sit next to them in an adjacent chair. The three of them immediately had a robust conversation started.

Samuel was absent but Sergei knew he would be in his bedroom working on some deal or another. He seemed busier than ever the last few days and Sergei guessed he had some big deals in the offing. Like having promised compositions unfinished as their deadlines approached.

The two young students were looking younger than ever. The kids, Kirk and Claire, were in position with their instruments and providing entertainment with quiet selections that featured them both and the festivities going around them. Sergei went to the piano and sat there turning so he could watch the goings on. It suddenly became quiet and everything seemed to have stopped, even the activity in the kitchen. All were looking his way and waiting.

He turned toward the kids and they nodded their heads in unison. Sergei began his Trio Elegiaque. It was as before and dinner was delayed for fifteen minutes.

The big table could handle eight so the kids would use trays and sit in the living room but close enough to feel included. Almost every dish and utensil in the house were in use, the table was dressed in festival finery and no better table could be imagined. It was to be an American Christmas dinner at it's best.

Goose was a replacement of turkey and was sided with tenderloin of beef. It was golden brown with a crispy skin and Samuel quickly, and expertly, handled the carving. A bowl of thyme and chestnut roasted potatoes and another of special carrots were ready. From Leokadiya's kitchen arrived a plate of just out of the oven dinner rolls, a large platter of roasted Brussels sprouts with cranberries and walnuts. Two pies, a pecan and an apple, with a side plate of assorted cheese slices were provided by the Korsakovs.

The plates were filled and a quiet descended for this fine meal being shared by what had become a small group of close friends. It was an excellent dinner as were the pies served with the cheese and coffees.

Samuel stood and made the speakers request by tapping his fork on a crystal glass. Having their attention he again thanked his guests for the enjoyable gathering and said he would like to talk to them about something that had come to his attention during the last few years that he thought he should share with them.

"First, you should understand why I have been here and what I have been doing. I am a free lance detective looking for trends and opportunities for American businessmen to pursue here in Russia and also for any interesting possibilities in nearby Europe. There is nothing mysterious or illegal about any of this. As an example, several American companies are developing the gasoline powered tractor for farming equipment. They want to know if there is a market here and how to approach it." Samuel stopped for a moment and was pleased to see even the kids were showing interest.

"How does this affect those of you here? It doesn't directly, but my conclusion that I am offering my clients does." Again he paused, then continued, "Timing is everything in business, and in life's pursuits. To be successful you must be in the right place, at the right time, and have the abilities required. Many places are the right place. Having the ability like composing a concerto can be an example. Sergei, I think the time is right for you. This is the place. Take advantage of this. Now!"

Some laughter was a good sign for Samuel and he continued, "I have reported to my American tractor manufactures this is not the right time or place for them to build factories here. Pay the shipping costs on your American built equipment and keep you production in America."

Again he paused, then finished his thought, "All the people I have contacted in the manufacturing sector here are beginning to worry about rebellious rumblings in their workers attitudes, as well within the poor and peasantry. Even more so within the recently retired military solders. There seems to be some discontent rising in the university students in a variety of social levels. It is just starting here in Saint Petersburg but revolutions always end badly. When, and if, this will happen I have no idea but I think it may become apparent in the next few years.

"Tsar Nicholas II will have his problems. No doubt the trend will be toward socialism, either ending up as communism or as fascism. It will take time to develop, maybe ten to fifteen years, but as you see it progress you should take whatever means you can to protect what is yours and yourself. Just keep this in mind for now but think about coming to America, with your family, if it starts happening here."

Samuel took his seat and Rose handed Sergei a wrapped package. Cynthia started laughing, then told him, "Mom and I found this in a pawn shop a few weeks ago and we could see it could be restored a bit and make a good music sheet travel case. It turned out nice, don't you think? Wait till you see who once owned it."

Sergei's hands began to shake and he looked toward his Mother. "This was my Father's," was whispered by Sergei. V.A.R. was stamped just below the handle.

Sergei had handed his small gift to Cynthia at the same time and she had been opening it as she talked about the music case. When she saw the locket she was taken aback by how pretty it was and then on a closer inspection realized it must contain something special.

Lyubov causally mentioned to her that it held Sergei's baby locks and Cynthia's eyes betrayed her thoughts and her tears became uncontrollable.

There was now total confusion in the room. The youngsters had no idea what was going on and Sergei was at a loss of what he should do next as he sat with his father's music case in his lap and watched helplessly as Cynthia seemed to have collapsed with her head being cradled in his mother's lap. The Korsakovs sat quietly together observing a scene they had seen before over their many years and were waiting for Samuel to take the lead.

He took his daughter's hand and pulled her up, turned toward Sergei beckoning him to follow them into Cynthia's bedroom. He closed the door behind them and with a faint smile said, "Merry Christmas."

Sergei set the case down on the bed and sat down next to it. Samuel had Cynthia sit down next to Sergei and he stood in front of them.

"I gave you my time and place speech already but this is where we are, the three of us. The time is no longer right for me, and neither is the place. My work is done here and I need to get back home to Cleveland to start anew before it is too late for me. Sergei, as I just said to you minutes ago, this is your time, this is your place. You must take advantage of it as it seldom happens this way, and sometimes it never does."

Samuel then took his daughter into his arms and softly spoke to her as if they were alone. "This is not your time. Understand this. Anything you involve yourself with Sergei now will not end well. If it is ever to happen it will be at another time and in another place. It is not now, not here!"

He went to the door, but before opening it, said to Sergei, "Show her your lock of hair. How to take care of it and then kiss her good evening."

Chapter 44
2022

The translated copies of the letters had been distributed among the group. It took only reading the first few to detect the pattern of Sergei's style and many matched the known writings compiled in the previous biographies. It wasn't until his letter dated 19 May 1902, one week after his marriage to Natalia Satina, that they took on a very different tenor.

How can I, a married man of only one week, write a love letter to another woman? I can't, I shouldn't, no descent man would, but I sit here at my little desk in my little room alone doing just that.

"Thin like a stick, Black like a raven, Maiden Natalka, I pity you," I would tease my Natalia when we were young. How mean a little boy was I then. She is neither thin as a stick or black like a raven but is a beautiful young woman whom I am falling in love with. She is smart, talented and loves me. I can ask for nothing more.

But dear Cynthia it was you and your love that brought my confidence back and removed the dark gloom of despair which I was sinking into at the time. When you left me alone on the station platform watching the last car disappear down the track words tumbled through my mind of my broken heart and I could at the same time hear the music needed to set them to. During the month before my wedding, desperately needing some income to pay for a honeymoon, it was like that and I wrote twelve songs, two in one day alone. My publisher bought them and paid me on the spot. Tomorrow we head to Italy for a three month honeymoon.

Thank you, thank you, thank you. Three were written for you and you will know which ones, not by a dedication but by the content.

Kiss me goodnight, tonight.

Seryozha

John and Allison had taken the sheath of letters to bed with them and he was glancing at the dates and salutations without much interest while she had read the 19 May 1902 twice.

She handed it to him and watched him read. She enjoyed these minutes watching his concentration and admired the speed and care he took. It was the same no matter what he was doing. Buttering a piece of toast or scanning a lengthy technical document. She knew the toast would be perfectly buttered and the document would be thoroughly understood.

He rolled over on his side towards her, letting his hand slide onto her shoulder, saying, "Our friend does have a problem here but we already know how it is worked out. Wilma is right, saying he was such a nice man. I think I am beginning to like him more and more and would have liked to have had him as a friend."

John got out of bed, retrieved one of the reference books from the table and sat next to Allison on her side of the bed. Thumbing through the pages he found what he was looking for, cleared his throat and started reading.

Cynthia's Dreams

"If for a whole month one sees something every day, no matter what, no matter how interesting, city, cathedral, gallery, the dungeons in the palazzo of the doges, all finally grows confused, insipid, boring, and then, of course, fatigue sets in. A fatigue that drives you into some room and keeps you there for at least a week, so pleasant it is to look at bare walls and any hint of a Madonna or a ruin would madden you."

Allison was laughing, smiling and reached for John. "His honeymoon. How awful to be taken out of your environment like that and into becoming a tourist. He is the creator of what we need to fulfill our lives, not being the observer of other's creations."

Robert and Sandra were in the guest bedroom in John's house which had become almost a second home for them. They also had the newly copied Rachmaninoff letters and were doing the same thing John and Allison had been doing. Casually reading letters at random as their curiosity guided them.

Sandra commented first, "Oh my God, Robert, this was written on 21 May, 1903. One week after his first daughter was born. Irina. He writes that she is a perfect little bundle and that he had just held her for the first time. He had been afraid to even touch her as she was so small and he felt so clumsy with his big hands. Natalia and her mother teased him like young girls might until he relented. Irina looked at him, into his eyes and then smiled. He writes to Cynthia that he knew at that moment he would never be able to say no to her no matter what she might ask of him."

Sandra put the letter down and looked at Robert. They exchanged looks for a few moments when Sandra said,"You will never have the chance to experience that feeling. At least with me as a mother."

"I want nothing in my life to be other than what it has been or what it is now. Nothing different," Robert answered as he reached for her hand.

Sandra smiled the smile he cherished and moved the letter to where he could see the headings. There was a second date, 26 August 1903.

"Read this part. He didn't finish the first part of the letter because of what happened after the family moved to their summer retreat in Ivanovka."

It's been long since I've had a bad a summer as this one and if I should describe it for you, there would be nothing to tell you but of illnesses. I was ill for almost half the summer, Natalia was very sick until July 15, and, finally, my little girl has also been sick up to two or three weeks ago. It has been possible for me to work only the past couple of weeks, but then I fell ill again, which kept me in bed all last week. Feel sorry for me Cynthia but be glad you are not here.

Robert handed the letter back to Sandra and gave her a weak smile. "Maybe we shouldn't read these letters but this is all leading us to what we suspect must have happened. All the pieces of the puzzle lay around us and it will make for a good story if we put them together correctly."

In the middle house Jennifer had lightly knocked on Wilma's bedroom door and opened it to look in on her. This had been become a nightly routine enjoyed by both. This night Wilma was propped up, wide awake, with her copies of Mr. Rach's letters.

"Jennifer come sit with me a bit. Reading these letter makes me feel like I am fifteen again and hearing him talk to me in person. He was such a nice man. I have told you that before, I am sure."

Jennifer sat by her side and marveled at the emotion she was feeling in reading the letters. She could imagine a fifteen year old girl, with the world famous musician talking to her in a fatherly manner.

"Let me read a little part of this letter, 16 June 1907." Wilma shuffled the two pages and started, "I'll begin by saying that my Natasha, thank God, is well and from day to day awaits my future son. . . ." Wilma stopping just long enough to emphasis what came next, "When my son comes on 21 June he turned out to be a daughter. The little girl has behaved rather decently for the first three days of her life. She sleeps far more than Irina did at the beginning, and cries less -- but when she does in a voice of thunder. Natasha now feels perfectly well. We're naming the little girl Tatiana."

Jennifer clasped Wilma's hand and kissed her on both cheeks, and said, "What beautiful thoughts to go to sleep with. Tomorrow will be another fine day for us all," leaving before Wilma could see her tears.

When Jennifer entered her and Ben's room she found him asleep with the opened Bertensson & Leyda Rachmaninoff book laying on his chest. She carefully lifted it and marked his place. She changed into her nightgown and slipped in next to this remarkable man that had given the last half of her life such meaning.

The first half had been as the wife of a Naval Top Gun pilot, then after that the move into a top secret test pilot stationed in Fallen, Nevada. Her move from the high adrenal atmosphere of jet fighter pilots into the world of musicians had been a dramatic change and one she now cherished above all that had happened before in her life. The tiny, ten dollar part that failed in the Mach Two engine at 20,000 feet above Fallen that afternoon had taken her husband's life in one second and she now was with another whose life was passing, day by day, solving the biggest and smallest of life's problems with a seeming ease that she admired every bit of as much as those in the pulse racing atmosphere of her past.

Ben stirred slightly as she made herself comfortable next to him and accepted her finger tip touch on his cheek.

In the third house, Ed and Julia's, it was totally different. Ed and Cindy were working together on Rachmaninoff's Symphony Number 5. Cindy had the piano portion completely memorized with that uncanny knack that concert pianists have for memorization. Ed was reading the instrumental music as she played and had come to the realization he could now hear in his mind what it should sound like. He was becoming a conductor as well as a pianist. They would pick a starting point in the movement and as Cindy played through her part he could read what the various orchestra contributions should be. The entrance, sound, volume and tonal qualities. Repeat, repeat and memorize. That the composer could write this music with only the mind and pencil continued to amaze him and it hadn't been until Ed had begun to hear what was written that he had had any idea how Rachmaninoff could have done it.

This afternoon, and then after dinner that evening,

Julia had been reading the letters and watching as her husband and the beautiful young pianist went through their practice. She remembered the period when they were partners as entertainers and how Ed was able to accompany her singing so effortlessly that it had sometimes taken her breath away. They had worked together, produced a number of number one hits and for ten years it had provided them wealth beyond their needs.

She could see this partnership developing between Ed and Cindy and knew it would also develop between him and the orchestra members. He had a gift to quietly be a part of an other's life that made many of the trials that came seem to never have occurred.

As the evening's practice in the third house came to an end all headed to bed and a quiet had descended. Ed and Julia lay close together, exchanged an unsaid message of contentment with each other and sleep came easily for both of them.

Cindy and BJ had found a similar unity that satisfied their desires and they too were soon asleep.

In another time and in another place, other lives were being lived. The two people who were responsible for what was happening now in Palm Desert were living the lives that would merge and make the possibility for what was now happening there.

Chapter 45
2022

The next morning all had gathered for breakfast around the pool and on this morning each had fixed what they wanted from what was available in Ben's kitchen. It was another Palm Desert morning and was so comfortable they all did what was required, sitting in lounge chairs, lounging.

It was Ben that started the conversation. "I have been reading Sergei Rachmaninoff, A Lifetime In Music by Bertensson and Leyda and found a short piece I would like to read to you." Ben said this, looking around and saw their interest. Wilma asked that he please do as she wanted to hear stories about her beloved Mr. Rach.

"This was a reminiscences of Nikolia Teleshov who hosted a gathering at his home for the opera singer Fyodor Chaliapin. It was in the autumn of 1904."

Ben had opened the book he was holding, finding his place and began reading the text.

"I remember one remarkable evening in the autumn of 1904. It was to be a big day. Gorky, the famous socialist writer had arrived in Moscow and was coming, Chaliapin was going to sing. And indeed the place was packed. And Chaliapin, the minute he got in, said joyfully, Brothers I want to sing. He telephoned Rachmaninoff and said, Seryozha, I am just dying to sing. Take a cab and hop around quick. We'll sing all night. Rachmaninoff was soon there. Chaliapin did not even give him time for tea. He sat him down at the piano, and something very wonderful began. This was at the height of Chaliapin's fame and powers. He was in an exceptional fine mood and sang literally without pause. There were no readings that evening, nor could there be. He was inspired. Never anywhere at any time was he so magical as he was that night. He himself said, several times, this is where you should hear me, not at the Bolshoi. Chaliapin fired Rachmaninoff, and Rachmaninoff set Chaliapin on fire, and these two, urging each other on, achieved miracles. This was not music or singing as anyone had ever known it. It was the inspired ecstasy of two great artists. I still see that great room, lit by a single hanging lamp above them, all eyes looking one way, at the piano where Rachmaninoff sat, at his black-coated back and the nape of his neck and his clipped hair. His elbows move swiftly, his long thin fingers strike the keys, and against the wall, facing us, a tall fine figure of a man, Chaliapin. He is in high boots and light black Russian coat of a fine woven material, one hand rest lightly on the piano, his face tense, not a glimmer left now of the just uttered jest. He waits for the moment of his first notes, he is transformed into the character whose soul he is to open before us, to let us feel the things it feels, know the things it knows."

Ben folded the book on his lap and nodded toward his audience. "I have read this three times now and I can see the room, smell the air, hear the music, and wish only that I could have been there. This does not often happen in ones life, when people of superior talent show it so completely to a small group of friends. I wish I had been there."

It was Cindy that stood up and came over to sit by Ben. She took his hands in hers and said in a whisper, but that all could hear, "That was how my dreams were. Sitting next to Sergei I could sense every detail of him, just as you described what you could imagine. I want to experience it again. At least once more."

Then a more serious look came to her face. "I have had that experience, that was described as being on fire. It is not what you are thinking. It is playing beyond your ability. Having complete confidence that you are doing every thing perfect. Effortlessly and perfect. For both Sergei and Fyodor, to have been at that level all evening, would indeed be a miracle."

She then quietly said, "Ed does this as he conducts. Everyone in the orchestra knows he knows their parts and will bring them in exactly on time with the right emphasis of volume and tone. It is so good to be part of this. So good to be part of his family."

Cindy couldn't hide her emotions any longer, went to BJ and asked him to take her to their room. The rest watched their beautiful new daughter leave and all realized what she had brought into their lives.

Chapter 46
1900-1909

The next week sped by and all Sergei could do was watch the happenings. The piano crew was there most of the day as Cynthia's piano was prepared for shipping back to America. The lid, legs, arbor and music rack were removed and wrapped. The case prepared and with a special block and tackle arrangement on the roof was slid out through the tall street side window and lowered to the sidewalk. It was loaded into a truck with all the other wrapped parts and the planks that had been used in crating the piano in New York, just over two years ago.

Suddenly all went quiet in the Beckman's apartment. Cynthia couldn't control her emotions any longer and with no hesitation went into Sergei's arms. Her parents went into their bedroom and left them alone together.

"I will never forget you and we will somehow be together again. I have to think that will happen. Promise me when we meet again it will be as it is now between us. It doesn't make any sense to think this way but I need something to hold on to." Cynthia said this still in Sergei's arms and not wanting to move. He was having the same problem and was having trouble telling her what he wanted to say to her.

"Some how we will be together again. It will happen and my feelings for you will be stronger than even now. I will write every time I have something good to tell you and in one letter it will be the one that tells you when and where we will be together again. I promise it will happen. It has to as I must know what might of have been. Not just think how it might have been, but know what it would have been."

Three days later, Wednesday January 6, 1900 the Beckman apartment was empty and Sergei Rachmaninoff made his plans to return to Moscow, to be married to Natalia and start a new life that would define him as one of the greatest pianist, composer and conductor Russia had ever produced.

In the morning the Beckmans, and Sergei, had made the trip to the train station by carriage with a half dozen bags carrying all that had not been shipped back to Cleveland. Much of the remaining items collected during three years by the family had been distributed among the apartment dwellers and what was left was taken to a charity house. It was the memories that would be taken to America, or left here in Russia, that were the heaviest burden.

Cynthia was having the most problems at their parting and after one last embrace and kiss left Sergei and boarded the compartment for the trip to Dresden, the first stop on their way home. She sat next to the window but did not look up, her head was down, her eyes closed trying to stop the tears that refused to stop coming.

Her father had taken Sergei's hand and took him aside. "Sergei, I have mentioned this to you before but please listen to me. Things are starting to move in a very bad direction here. It will not threaten you as much as most because of your intrinsic value to Russian society is too important. Writer's such as Maksim Gorky are becoming popular and Vladimir Lenin's name is becoming familiar to to the masses. These are socialists, communists, and following in their path will be catastrophic. Don't be fooled into associating with them, or the Bolsheviks. They are idealist and, as with all idealist, will make everyone around them unhappy. Stick with your music and give the world what it needs, not what what some bureaucrats tells you that you must do."

The last boarding call was made and Sergei Rachmaninoff then stood alone on the platform, unhappy, confused and shoulders bent. As the last car of the train disappeared from view he still stood motionless, the day had turned gray, a light snow had started falling and the coldness of his world began seeping into his being.

The last porter on the platform walked past Sergei pushing an empty cart. He stopped, turned around and approached him. "That's the last train today. You better head back inside as the weather is going to get worse. Come with me and I'll treat you to a coffee." Gorgei Mastroni spent an hour with a man he didn't know but helped at the moment when he needed it most. Sergei remembered that kindness and many times in the future, when thing were going poorly for him, he would think of having a cup of coffee and good conversation with that complete stranger.

The next morning he was back at the station waiting to board the train to Moscow. He had come early to see if he could find Gorgei Mastroni and thank him for what he had done for him the day before. Not only could he not find him, none of the other porters knew the name or recognized Sergei's description. The last call was made for the train to Moscow and he just made it into the second class car in time. His mother had paid for his ticket and he was relieved to have a window seat with only one other passenger in the compartment.

He then began thinking what had happened over the last two weeks. Natalia had told him of her love for him and started his thinking that she should be his choice for a wife and mother of his children. Before that thought had a chance to grow into a reality the Beckman family entered his life and he fell hopelessly in love with Cynthia Beckman. Her promises of what was possible for them were still in his thoughts, pushing out all other rational thinking as to his future. And then to send his mind into absolute chaos this morning saying goodbye to Leokadiya Kashperova she pulled him to her and made an obvious offer that anytime he wanted to she had a place in her bed for him to stay when in Saint Petersburg.

He watched the country side go by, wiping the moisture off the glass with his coat sleeve as it formed. The winter scene was beautiful looking at it from the warmth inside the compartment. He tried to clear his thoughts of everything other than the scenery. The ride was smooth and almost silent with just the faint rhythm of the wheels on the rails. A poem came to mind, although he couldn't remember the words or the author. It could be put to music and the notes were forming in his mind. At that moment all else left his thoughts and he reached for the music case that had once been his father's, opened it and reached for a pencil and a music sheet.

The announcement came for arrival in Moscow and he stuffed the twelve pages of sheet music back into the case and with a smile, reached for his suitcase knowing most of his problems were now behind him. He knew what he was meant to do and that he could do it.

Chapter 47
1900-1909

The next nine years were a defining period in Sergei Rachmaninoff's life. It started with his daily sessions with the esteemed Dr. Dahl. In the same apartment building as his small room in the Satin's home it was located just a short walk between the floors. For over two months they talked each day of things big and small. Even though Sergei knew he had already recovered from his depression thanks to the love given him by Cynthia Beckman and with the help she and Leokadiya Kashperova in finishing the first movement of his Concerto Number 2.

His talks with Dr. Dahl had improved his sleeping by the quieting of his mind when sleep was required. Waking refreshed was a help and whenever the problem came about he would recite the teachings of the good doctor. He, however, never told him about the two weeks he had spent with Cynthia and her parents. There was some gossip about the gatherings with Rimsky-Korsakov in attendance and the fabulous music that had been played. They talked about that a number of times as Dr. Dahl was a talented musician.

A cousin, Alexander Siloti tens years older than Sergei, would play an important part in his life during this period. And even more important was another cousin, Natalia Satina, four years his junior who would become his wife, bear him two daughters and provide a stable life in which he would thrive. Her younger sister, Sofia, would also be with them throughout the rest of his life and afterward make a name for herself in science. Their mother, Varvara Satina, was most important in making the things happen that were needed to insure his future.

Most notable was the composition and orchestration of Rachmaninoff Concerto Number 2, which at the time of the debut was only the second and third movements in December of 1900 and was dedicated to Dr. Nikolai Dahl. It was performed complete for the first time on 27 October 1901 with Sergei as the pianist and Siloti as conductor of the Moscow Philharmonia Society. Dahl was again given credit for lifting Sergei out of his depression to finish this masterwork but there were a few who knew when and with who's help that the first movement had been completed.

In April 1902 he composed his Twelve Songs in a few short weeks, while at Ivanovka, to pay for his upcoming honeymoon, He had several paying jobs, one for two years as the conductor for the Bolshoi Theater in Moscow. Another as a teacher at the St. Catherine's and Elizabeth schools, more popularly known as the Two Girls School, where he had been adored by his young students and was financially rewarded as well. His life was coming together and the birth of his first daughter brought a guiding light into his very being.

As the new year of 1905 came so did Bloody Sunday on January twenty-second in Saint Petersburg. The shooting by the Tsar Nickolas II's guards into the demonstrators as they marched towards the Winter Palace set into motion what would become a revolution in 1917. A number of concessions calmed the atmosphere at the time but the intelligentsia, including Rachmaninoff, added to the disdain of the Tsarists rules.

The composition of the Isle of the Dead, inspired by a black and white reproduction of a painting by Arnold Bocklin, was a Rachmaninoff masterpiece of death as the final aspect of life. This was in mi-April of 1909 and he later said if he had seen the original painting in color he would have never written it.

The trip to America was still in doubt at this time and the delays by the twenty day round trip for corresponding caused more concern. The family had been in residence in Dresden, Germany for the last three years and he had just returned to Moscow as the negotiations continued. He received notice by cable that his impresario had died and his family would carry on with the negotiations. In haste he sent back the signed contact hoping they would cancel the whole thing as he didn't really want to do the tour. He then received notice from New York the contract had been accepted and $2500 deposited in his name for the last five concerts. "So he made it. Maybe his impresario had died of chagrin," was Rachmaninoff's thought.

Sergei had been working on a third concerto to be premiered on this tour and he now set out on a rushed composition of his Third Concerto. He finished it just in time to board the ship to America and had to practice using a silent keyboard he had brought with him.

He arrived in New York on October 26, exhausted and fearing the tour he had just committed to. He had one last hope and that was that he could hire a secretary to take care of all his paperwork and that he could make enough money to buy a car. He didn't know how to drive and had no idea of how to manage a secretary but needn't have worried as everything would work out just fine. This part of his story would now become the part of Cynthia Beckman's life that he would never, at least not for many years, know about.

Chapter 48
1900-1909

For the Beckmans life was not so easy or pleasant. They arrived in Cleveland exhausted, uncertain of their futures and in Cynthia's case, unhappy and broken hearted. It had taken almost two full months with the three stops, in Dresden, Warsaw and Paris, for them to finally reach home.

In Dresden, although a beautiful city and nice to tour, Samuel's business meetings were unproductive and for the first time he was beginning to think it had been a mistake to put in so much effort helping his clients when what he saw coming in this part of the world would not lead to more commerce for them. Warsaw was the same as Dresden, enormously bigger in size and architecture and didn't seem nearly as friendly.

Paris was Paris and he had no business dealings there so they spent two weeks being American tourist. They did a good job at that and even Cynthia had a few smiles to give others. Twice she played a piano for their dinner and politely turned down offers to make the rest of her life a dream if she would merely spend a single night with the rather inebriated gentlemen making the offers.

Leaving from Liverpool after two nights in London found them in New York in six more days and back to Cleveland three days later.

Samuel had had a house built for them on East

108th Street, just a few blocks from the University Circle area and Case Western Reserve University. It was becoming a world class cultural center and a number of nice homes were being built along the well laid out streets. It was a two story, four bedroom, three bath house with a large living room, separate dining room and a modern kitchen. He even had a garage built, with room for two cars, in anticipation for the future of the automobile manufacturing potential that he was predicting for Cleveland.

The opportunity for Samuel to represent several large companies looking at the business climate in Russia for markets for their new agricultural equipment seemed to have been a good idea at the time. He spoke several languages, including Russian, and could read and write in most of them. It ended up that the conclusions he came to about the political landscape were in opposition to financial benefit coming his way.

He had set up a rental arrangement with Case to rent the four bedrooms out on six month leases such that the new staff that was coming into the expanding University would have good living accommodations as they came from various points across America. The lease was set up until the last day of 1899. The University would clean, make repairs and replace any damaged items to have the house as new on March 1, 1900.

They arrived on Thursday, March 8th, exhausted and not really functioning rationally. A carriage brought them from the train station to their address where they had only resided for a few months before leaving for Saint Petersburg, Russia. They were now entering their house as strangers. With the five bags placed on the porch, Samuel took out the house key he had carried in his pocket for the last three years and inserted into the lock. The latch clicked, the door knob turned and they walk into the house. In the foyer Rose put her arm around Cynthia's waist and Samuel drew the two of them to him. It was quiet in the house, it looked clean and also smelled that way. On the foyer table was a big bouquet of flowers and a small welcome home sign. It had been signed by a number of names they didn't recognize but later found they were by all the young teachers that had stayed there over the three years with personal thank you notes from each.

The tears came and it was ten minutes before they moved. They had furnished the house before they had left and as they headed toward the living area they saw a few pieces that were different but most were the original ones and in like new condition. There was one item that had not been there before, a Steinway Model C Parlor Grand Piano. They went to it and Cynthia sat down on the bench and pushed back the fall board as Samuel lifted the lid and placed the strut. The piano glistened in the semi-dark room and time seemed to have stopped. Cynthia placed her fingers on the keys and played Rachmaninoff Number 2 Second Movement and then on through to to the end of the Third.

They were home and Sergei Rachmaninoff had come with them.

Chapter 49
1900-1909

The four bedrooms were on the second floor. The small room at the top of the stairs was converted to become Samuel's office. The master suite, with a sitting room and full bathroom, was on the back side of the house. The third bedroom, which was for Cynthia, was on the opposite corner from Samuel's office and was a large room with its own full bathroom. The fourth bedroom was very small and would be used as a small den with a single bed bolstered to be used as a couch. It did have a door access to Cynthia's bathroom which was to later come in handy. The layout made the master suite and Cynthia's room isolated enough to make them private. Even the bathrooms were laid out with no common wall.

Downstairs was likewise well designed and the living room was large, seemed designed for the Parlor Grand piano, and had the space to seat two dozen when needed. The dining room was large and the table could seat ten with ease. The kitchen was the best 1900 could offer. A small room with sink and toilet was strategically placed off a hallway. Samuel Beckman had been the architect.

Fortunately the house had been built and paid for in full from an inheritance from Rose's parents. The three years of rents, though modest, had paid all expenses associated with the house and had a small profit left over.

Cynthia's Dreams

It took the family a week to settle into their new life in Cleveland. It became apparent that what Samuel had expected in bonus monies from the dozen companies he represented was far less than he had expected. The value of his recommendations not to move any manufacturing into Russia, Germany or Poland, would not become obvious to his clients until later. Two decades later they would realize they would have lost all of their investments and possibly even their lives if they had not taken his advice. Two had decided to compete in the automobile business as Europe had been ahead by a few years in design and production but then watched as their facilities were confiscated and others destroyed. Samuel was paid no bonus monies for this valuable foresight and he was now left to start something new to support his family.

He shouldn't have worried as a man of his talents would always find something that he could do that had value for others. But it would be Cynthia and Rose that led the way this time and it happened as many good fortunes do, unplanned and by surprise.

Rose's first love was reading. She was fluent in several languages, had studied literature in college and had a degree in English Literature from Vassar. Her grandmother, Elizabeth Proxmire, had willed to Rose her only prized possession, her book collection.

Rose ventured out to the University to inquire as to the possibility of employment as a teacher. She didn't have time to pursue this, however, as her mentioning she was a Vassar graduate had her meeting Adella Prentiss. She happened to be standing next to her, as she made this first disclosure of her resume, and would have to pursue a teaching position later.

Adella was tall, very attractive and in her early thirties, nine years older than Cynthia. In those nine years she had followed her love of music and travel and at this time was trying to help restart the just failed effort to bring a symphony orchestra to Cleveland. In the quick conversation about graduating from Vassar with a literature degree, a daughter who was a pianist and a husband that was a multi-talented business executive had Rose and Cynthia invited for lunch the next day. The small French cafe one block from where they stood was suggested, pointed out and the time was agreed to be at 11:30 am. A handshake and Adella Prentiss was on her way to wherever she was then needed. Rose had remained watching her exit as if rooted to the floor. A smile came to her face as she knew at that moment something good was going to happen tomorrow.

Samuel's office had a view to the street and for the last few days he had sat in his big chair, behind his big desk, looking out at the street. He was almost paralyzed as he realized that he had no prospects to pursue, no income to expect and suddenly seemingly no future. He didn't want to think that way. He had never been in that position before.

Downstairs Cynthia sat at the piano. Occasionally she would place her hands in position and play a short melody. They were sad, forlorn pieces that expressed her feelings. They were new compositions, well composed but they just came to her and then were gone, not to be remembered.

Samuel coming downstairs broke her concentration and she looked toward her father. She knew he was having a bad time right now and it was hard on both her mother and her to see him this way. He only said, "The mail is here and something came," and he rushed out the door. Returning he came over to Cynthia and gave her the envelop. It was of heavy, brown paper, was from Russia and addressed to Cynthia Beckman in strained, but legible English handwriting.

"A letter from Sergei Rachmaninoff, I believe," was said as he handed the letter to his daughter.

Chapter 50
1900-1909

Cynthia took the letter from her father, looked at the addressing and with a look of fear ran upstairs to her bedroom. Shutting the door behind her she laid down on her bed and starred intently at the addressed envelope. It was his handwriting. It was the letter he had promised to write and it had been over two months since she last saw him, kissed him and told him she loved him. It was five minutes before she took the letter opener and carefully slit the envelope open.

The letter was two pages and written in Russian. It was dated 17 February 1900. If he had mailed it the day it was written it had taken three weeks to arrive. She read it through twice, then just held it and thought about its content. He missed her and wanted her back in his life. He was keeping their relationship a secret, telling no one and was keeping his own secret, that she had brought him out of his depression and he was ready to compose again. Then about his visit, with Fyodor, to Tolstoy and that it had been a disaster. He was continuing with his unnecessary appointments with Dr. Dahl and about their conversations. That her sending her mail to him through Leokadiya would work out. Then about the engagement to Natalia Satina and the plans for his marriage. His last sentence was, "Before you fall asleep tonight, kiss me once more. I love you."

She blotted the tear drops that had found the paper and carefully folded the two sheets to put them in the envelop. At the last minute she changed her mind and got the letter paper box she had in her desk. It was the same paper size and she took out the few remaining sheets and placed her two Rachmaninoff ones in the box. She would let her mother read it later, and then also her father. At this moment she would keep her love affair to herself.

Rose had returned excited by who she had just met and that a lunch date had been arranged for tomorrow to continue a conversation she knew was going to mean a lot for all three of them. The house was silent, as if no one was there and a sense of fear crept into her mind.

Going up stairs she looked in on Samuel and he was seated at his desk starring out the window. He had set up his office efficiently using all the space available. There were two big stuffed chairs for guests and as she entered he sensed her presence and stood up to greet her. He always did that and came to her and kissed her. He had been the only man that had ever kissed her and she had never wanted another.

She sat in one of the chairs as he returned to his and started by telling her about the letter from Sergei, that Cynthia had taken it up to her room.

"I have something to tell you and you should know about this first. I just met Adella Prentiss. Cynthia and I have been invited to lunch with her tomorrow at eleven thirty. I don't know who she is but she went to Vassar and appears to own most of the world. At least here in Cleveland."

Rose had to pause as she generally was not a talker

but before Samuel could respond she continued, "Why don't you find out who she is and why she would be so interested in us. I was talking to someone about getting a teaching position and mentioned I had graduated from Vassar and that our daughter was a pianist. Vassar and pianist were the trigger and I don't think I said anything else to her until I said we would delighted to join her for lunch."

Samuel sat still, observing his wife. She was still, at fifty, a beautiful woman. Intelligent in many ways exceeding his, and the only woman he had ever loved. Her intuition had never disappointed either of them and what she said next was what he needed at that moment.

"I think we will find something for all three of us here with this woman. She is about thirty, I think, but exudes a confidence of a person that gets things done. Big things. Something exciting is going on, fun and that we can share. It may not be financially what we need, but let's find out. You need to find out who she is."

Rose left Samuel with his new project and went across the upstairs landing to Cynthia's bedroom door and knocked. She answered and immediately hugged her mother. Rose could see she had been crying and asked if it had been something in Sergei's letter.

"You talked to Daddy about it. I haven't seen him since the mail came and he brought it to me. I came up here and I was afraid to open it. I did and all is fine and for some reason I am happy for him and not sorry for myself. I will let you read it later. It took three weeks to get here."

It seemed to Rose that Cynthia wanted to leave it at that so she told her about meeting Miss Prentiss and the lunch date tomorrow. That Samuel was going to find out who this young woman was and why she was so anxious to have them meet with her the next day.

At dinner that evening, Rose served a simple soup and salad. The conversation had started as the meal was served and Samuel told Rose and Cynthia what he had been able to find out. It had a required a short walk to the campus and the cost of two cups of coffee at the school lounge. It appeared everyone on the campus knew who Adella Prentiss was, the woman who would later become The Mother of the Cleveland Orchestra.

Chapter 51
1900-1909

Rose and Cynthia entered the Petite Cafe at exactly 11:30 am and were greeted by an attractive young woman who asked them to come with her as their table was ready. Adella would arrive shortly as she was always a little late. She spoke with a pronounced French accent and when Rose answered her in perfect French the conversation became more animated and when Cynthia joined in the entire room began watching the scene unfold. The owner and chef, Andre Pelletier, came out of the kitchen and things got even more exciting as Adella had arrived. She knew immediately what had happened and thought that this family, just back from an extended stay abroad, were who she needed at this moment to get things moving with her current projects. She would not be disappointed.

Lunch was served quickly and was delicious roasted chicken with wild rice and string beans. A basket of Paris quality croissants, butter and jam completed the table. Wine was offered but water was chosen. They sat the table for three hours and Adella was liking everything that was happening. Rose, Cynthia and Samuel were invited for that evenings gathering of the Fortnightly Club. The local string players would perform and she was sure they would find it an enjoyable evening.

The Beckmans arrived fifteen minutes early and were glad they had. Adella rushed up to greet them and immediate introductions to Johann Beck and Emil Ring were made. On the stage were eighteen musicians readying their instruments, adjusting seats and music stands in obvious preparations for a concert. In the middle of the stage stood a Steinway Model D Grand Piano, lid up and keyboard ready. It was all Cynthia could do not to run up to it and sit on the bench.

"Would you like to play us a little warm up as things get prepared," Adella asked Cynthia.

She didn't hesitate and walked up to the big piano. The stage was small and the space limited but she still manage to walk around it and admired how beautiful it looked. She had never had the chance to play a Model D before but was not intimidated. Sitting, she ran her fingers over the keys, pressed a few to get some feel for them and to her surprise felt totally confident.

Rose and Samuel watched and again were amazed at how confident their daughter had become with her music. The three years with Leokadiya Kashperova, Rimsky-Korsakovs, and finally Sergei Rachmaninoff had been life changing for their lovely daughter.

Johann Beck was the conductor for tonight's playing of Chopin's Piano Concerto Number 1 in E-minor. He had stepped to the podium and was rustling through the sheet music on his stand.

At that moment Cynthia started to play the two compositions she had given to Sergei. The gallery had filled with about two hundred, mostly music students and a number of Cleveland residents who would never miss the chance to hear classical music. The hall quieted immediately and almost everyone could hear Adella's panicked discussion with Beck that the pianist had not shown up.

The eighteen musicians, eleven violins, three violas, three cellos and one bass, were in place. Cynthia was just finishing her two pieces and the applause had started with "play them again" being asked for.

Johann Beck approached Cynthia and asked her if she knew Chopin Number One and she told him she had played it before but not in accompany of an orchestra. She asked for the sheet music and a page turner and said she thought she could do it. She played her two pieces a second time and this time all could enjoy what they were hearing, especially the musicians and Adella Prentiss.

Beck applauded her playing and was trying to think if he had ever heard them before. But that was for later and he gathered his group's attention with a few raps on the stand with his baton. Nodding to Cynthia she acknowledge she was ready and he led into the first movement with every musician participating.

Leokadiya had taken Cynthia to several concerts that featured this very piece so she was familiar how it was to be played. She waited as the music flowed over her and suddenly felt totally confident. It is four and a half minutes of great string music before the piano enters and it gave her time to be ready at the level needed. Another forty minute in full participation, only needing a glance at the music sheets to know where she was and what was coming next.

Rose was holding Samuel's hand tight and they could not believe what they were witnessing. Their beautiful daughter was playing at the highest level with no hesitation.

After a piano cadenza at about twenty minutes was the first separation of the movements. The second started with one of the quiet melodies that sets up the entry of strings and then the piano that all love about Chopin. By this time all doubt about their substitute piano artist was gone and everyone played the best they ever had. The audience knew and appreciated what was happening.

Cynthia's style was quiet in movement of elbows, allowing the positioning of hands, her long, slender fingers touching the keys almost effortlessly. A beautiful young women playing beautifully.

The concerto ends with one of the greatest piano cadenzas of all time and it did so this night.

A relationship was established that evening beween Adella Prentiss and the Beckmans that would last a lifetime. Samuel would become involved in many of her promotions of cultural events in and for Cleveland and Cynthia would become a friend and valued fellow pianist. The Beckmans were invited to her wedding to Felix Hughes in 1904 and would often be guests at social function held in their home, and then to her home after their divorce in 1923. She kept the last name Hughes and would be referred to as Adella Prentiss Hughes for the rest of her life.

Chapter 52
2022

John was sorting through the Rachmaninoff letters and had just finished reading the last one dated 18 June 1909. He found it the most interesting of the twenty-seven as it dealt with telling Cynthia Beckman much that was to change her life.

The Rachmaninoff family had spent the last three winter's in Dresden following the disturbances in Saint Petersburg and Moscow but would spend their summers at the Satin's estate of Ivanovka. Several of the earlier letters had described to Cynthia his recent performances as pianist and conductor appearances in Europe, Scandinavia, England and in Moscow and Saint Petersburg during the season of 1908 and the start of the 1909 one.

In this letter he described the delays in the planning of his first American tour which would be November of this year through January of 1910. The contract was still in limbo and just when he thought it would either happen, or not happen, the organizer Henry Wolfsohn, of the Wolfsohn Bureau, dies from pneumonia. Rachmaninoff signs the contract with his last remaining change included and sends it off to Henry's wife and daughter who are planning to keep the Wolfsohn Bureau in business. It was taking up to twenty days to round trip the contact papers and he had little hope of it happening.

In the letter he writes,

"There's something else - a secret. It is possible that this time, too, I shall not go to America. About ten days ago I received a cable about the death of my impresario. It said that the widow of the deceased along with some other people will take over my management. I wished to tempt fate once more, so I sent back my contract at once with a request for all these people, including the wife, to endorse the contract, which I added I would consider a sufficient guarantee.

Now I suppose they who receive this contract over there will rejoice at disposing so easily of at least one of the artist remaining on their hands, and will destroy my contract. To the Devil with it! I'll be inexpressibly happy! Incidentally a week ago I received notice from a New York bank that Wolfsohn had deposited there in my name, according to the contract, 2500 dollars, for the last five concerts. So he made it! Maybe he died of chagrin."

John had to smile at this. The idea of doing international business with a twenty day round trip correspondence would be such a burden that in modern business hardly anything could be accomplished.

The rest of the letter was of his date of arrival, the hotel he would be staying in and that he would need a secretary who could speak Russian. He told Cynthia he was sure he would be overwhelmed with so many Americans wishing to assist him and he would like to have at least one person he could be close to.

This brought another smile to John's face but what came next brought forth a laugh.

My dear Cynthia, how do I invite you back into my life at this time. I arrive in New York City on 26 October and I am sure I will be greeted by a mob of people I do not know or recognize. I will be escorted to a hotel I do not know and put in a room I have no idea of what it looks like.

I must see you again for many reasons as we have written in these letters over the years and I am still in love with you. It is wrong but please find a way for us to have some time together. I have several breaks in the current schedule and can make a trip to Cleveland to visit you and your mother and father there but that is not what I really want. Solve this problem for me. I will have little enough free time on this tour and I fear what it is going to be like. Save me once more

If my finances improve I want to hire a secretary and buy a car. Not there but when I get back. You could teach me how to drive. That would be a fun thing to do. I think of other things. Shame on me.

Be there somewhere.
I am silly and I am still in love with you,

SR"

John had started to laugh and then caught himself as the thought of a man as great as Rachmaninoff had become was still a young boy at heart. The teasing of Vera Skalon, the older provocative gypsy wife of an associate, and later a young ballerina who would challenge his good marriage to Natalia, with their two fine daughters. His love of Cynthia still found him in the uncomfortable position of an imagined love being put to a test in the reality of what would soon happen. John and the group were absolutely sure that he would father another daughter, this time with Cynthia Beckman, as the two of them would be together during his American tour. All that was left for the group was to follow that reality to their wonderful Cynthia Ashbaugh.

John heard piano and violin coming from the living room, closed up his office and quietly entered the room. Cindy was at the piano and Allison was next to the bench with the Venetian violin in position. They were both sight-reading from the score on the music rack and were playing a very nice duet together.

Another one of his almost now constant smiles came to his face as he watched the beautiful young pianist and the equally pretty violinist play a piece he had never heard before but wanted to hear many more times as the years went by.

Chapter 53
1909-1910

On Tuesday. October 26, 1909 Sergei Rachmaninoff arrived in New York City aboard the Kronprinzes Cecilie after a six day crossing from Bremen, Germany. A very tired and discouraged Sergei Rachmaninoff disembarked into a crowd of over five hundred people all cheering his arrival. He was met at the foot of the gangplank by Modeste Altschuler and asked him, in his best English, his first question on American soil, "When is the first rehearsal?"

He had a busy summer at Ivanovka, finishing The Isle of the Dead, getting it to the printers and composing and finishing his Third Concerto for piano and orchestra. Adding to all this was the negotiations of the contract for this American Tour. The preparations and travel back to Dresden from Ivanovka had also taken its toll as did leaving Natalia and his two small daughters behind in Russia.

The crowds, language and pushiness of the American press had him begging to get to the Netherland Hotel and to his room as soon as possible to hide.

Cynthia had arrived from Cleveland the night before and checked into her small room which was on the same floor as Rachmaninoff's suite. As she prepared to walk over to the docks that morning, she passed his suite's door and could hear a piano being played inside. Curiosity, and not being in a hurry, she knocked on the door. The piano playing stopped but no one came to the door. Another more aggressive knocking brought forth a short young man who took a long look at her and finally asked what she wanted as no one was here yet.

Cynthia answered that she had heard the piano being played, that she was a pianist and knew Sergei Rachmaninoff from ten years ago in Saint Petersburg when she had been a music student there. The young man smiled and again asked what she wanted.

"I would like to see the piano they have placed here for Sergei. I hope it is a Steinway Model D. When I knew him I had a Model C that my father had bought in New York and had shipped to Saint Petersburg for the time we were there. I helped him on the first movement of his Concerto Number 2," saying this in such an earnest manner that he let her come in. She went directly to the big grand piano.

Benedetto Santio introduced himself as the piano tuner sent over by Steinway to make sure the piano was in tune. They hoped placing it here would introduce him to their product and get them some business in the future.

Cynthia gave Benedetto the first of the many smiles he would be receiving from her over the next three months. She detected his Italian accent and carried on the conversation in his language for the next hour. Benedetto, twenty-three, fell in love with thirty-one year old Cynthia Beckman at that moment and made no objection to her sitting on the bench. She played the big piano with such skill he took a seat in one of the upholstered chairs, leaned back and listened.

She played the entire Concerto Number 2 for Piano, a number of his songs, and was just into the two pieces she had composed and given to Sergei when the door was opened and the entourage entered the room with the bedraggled Rachmaninoff being hustled about the suite by the hotel staff. Altschuler was rattling off the first of the schedule and several uninvited newspaper people added to Sergei's annoyance. All but Sergei had thought that the beautiful pianist had been hired to entertain their famous guest as a welcome to New York and they went about the seeing to it that he knew all he needed for his stay with them. The suite, and the piano, were for his use during the entire length of his stay in America.

Sergei paid no attention as he had gone immediately to the piano and said to Cynthia, "It is so good to see you here and to listen to you play again. I may survive the day yet. Please play some more while I try to find a way to get these people out of my room." He turned to Benedetto and in Italian mentioned that he must be the piano tuner Steinway said they would provide for the tour and that he should stay and protect Cynthia. The first smile in America showed on his face as he could see the short, young Italian had already fallen in love with her.

It took almost an hour to rid the suite of the hotel staff, Altschuler, his associates and the press. There were at least a dozen that shouldn't have been there in the first place. Everything Rachmaninoff was dreading about the tour was coming true in the first two hours he was here.

Cynthia tried to hide her emotions as the question of whether she would still have the love for Sergei after their ten year separation was answered in the first minutes they were together again. She waited to show any signs of her feelings for him until Benedetto excused himself, telling Rachmaninoff he had a room down the hall and that he was to accompany him on the tour as the piano tuner but that if there was anything else he could help him with was just to ask.

Sergei looked at Cynthia as Benedetto left the room, smiled and said, "There are two of us that are in love with you. One for only a few minutes so far and the other who still is since the day he first saw you."

Chapter 54
1909-1910

As Benedetto closed the door behind him Rachmaninoff approached Cynthia, reached for her hands and held them against his chest. He said nothing as he looked into her eyes. She made the first move and kissed him. It had all come back for them both as if it had been only yesterday they had last kissed each other.

"I am going to pass out if I don't get some rest. I can't remember ever being this tired and they want to me attend a welcome dinner tonight at eight. I am no good for you now," Sergei said, speaking slowly and in Russian,

Cynthia replied in kind, took him into the bedroom and had him lay down on the bed. She massaged his neck and shoulders and sang him a childish Russian song.

"I will wake you up at seven and you will have one hour to make yourself presentable. We will have time for ourselves when the time is right. We have no need to rush." As she had said this last he had fallen asleep.

Going back into the main room she looked about at where she was. It was a big room with windows overlooking the park. The trees were past their fall prime but the last of the colors presented a nice view. The big piano took up a good deal of space but the room was still large enough to not look crowded.

She found a comfortable chair, curled up in it with her head back on the cushion and closed her eyes. Her thoughts went back over the last ten years. They had arrived back in Cleveland tired but glad to be home. At least to their new house that was now three years older.

Her mother had made the contact with Adella Prentiss and the wheels of their future began turning. It was their both attending Vassar that had sparked the initial relationship between them and Cynthia's musical skills bonded the family even more. But Samuel was the key as his business contacts and relationships with the movers and shakers of the Ohio business community made him a natural fund raiser for Adella's vision for a Cleveland Symphony Orchestra and the other projects she was planning.

Rose secured a teacher's position in the English department and Cynthia found a seeming unending role in accompaniment and solo piano engagements that began to provide her some income. Samuel seemed to hit the big time quickly in raising funds for variety of big and small functions.

Between the three of them they had enough money to live comfortably and enjoy some fruits of their labor. Men came, and quickly went, in her life as none could compete with her memories of Sergei. Her father had purchased a car and all three had learned how to drive. The letter writing to Sergei had continued, although was slowing down as both their lives were starting to find success. The letter that had her here in New York City had been the last she had received and she thought it maybe would be the last one after the American Tour ended.

As she sat in the chair she started to wonder if what she was doing was a wise thing to do. She knew when Sergei went back to Russia he would be going home without her, taking only the memories of the affair. That she had no place in his future once he returned to his home, to his wife and to his children. She would not be a part of this and didn't think she should be. She would go back to her mother and father's home and live her life with them until what was to happen for her, happened. Until then she had but one object, to love Sergei Rachmaninoff until he could no longer be a part of her life and she would have to continue living on without him.

The big clock in the hall struck seven and she went into the bedroom to wake him. He reached for her and they lay together for a few minutes. She could feel his desire but he released her and sat up.

"I can't believe this is happening. You being here with me and we having some time to be together. I will do my duty to my sponsors and be back as soon a possible but it may be late. Maybe Benedetto can take you to a place for dinner. I will ask him to on my way downstairs. I better get ready," saying this last as he stood and looked down at her.

She smiled and asked, "Would you like me to be here when you come back after being with all those fawning fans. You will come back alone, I trust."

He gave Cynthia his hotel key and told her he would get a second key at the desk. She left him to clean up and get ready for this next performance. One which he dreaded but knew he must do. She went down the hall and knocked on Benedetto's door. They were soon seated at a small corner restaurant for a bowl of soup and sliced baguette. The soup was good as was the conversation.

Chapter 55
1909-1910

It was an enjoyable dinner, although simple, and the soup was excellent. Cynthia found Benedetto good company and a friendship was forming. The relationships between the three was openly discussed and understood.

They returned to Sergei's suite and Cynthia went to the piano and was poised to play when she noticed a folder that had been left on the music rack. She picked it up and opened it. It was a schedule for November's performances.

"Oh my God, Bennie! Can you believe this scheduling. Sergei has twelve events in November. They are all over the place. On the fourth Northampton, Massachusetts, on the eighth Philadelphia, Pennsylvania, the tenth Baltimore, Maryland, and the thirteenth here, fifteenth in Hartford, Connecticut, then Boston, Toronto, New York, Philadelphia again, then here for two more finishing on the thirtieth. They are trying to kill him!" Cynthia was almost in tears and Benedetto looked scared to death.

A quiet had filled the room and neither could think of what to say. It was Cynthia that broke the silence. "I am going to be his secretary and manager. I don't care if they have some one assigned already, he is going to need help and you are going to join me in this. Piano tuning will be the least of your chores. Are you with me?"

"Count me in. I didn't know what I was supposed

to do. Unless something is really wrong I didn't think I would have more than a few hours of work at each location. Then what was I supposed do?" was Benedetto's answer and he then added, "Bennie will be fine with me."

Cynthia played a few pieces and several parts of Concerto Number 3. Benedetto remarked that he had never heard that played before and Cynthia told him, "You are going to get to hear a lot of music you have never heard before. That part of this trip is going to be worth all the effort we make, seeing our man is properly taken care of."

It was 11:00 pm and Cynthia suggested that it was time for Bennie to head for his room and she was going to go to hers. They parted ways with the understanding that she would set up this effort for helping Sergei on his tour in the morning and that they would try to do something together that afternoon.

Cynthia was readying for bed when there was a knock on her door. It was 12:30 and she was in her nightgown but went to the door without donning her bathrobe. Sergei stood in the doorway but didn't try to come in. He stood and stared at the beautiful woman that was standing just in front of him and simply asked if she would join him for breakfast in the morning in his room. He bent his head down and mumbled that he could do no more this day and if he didn't answer in the morning to use her key and check to see if he had lived through his first day in America. And if he hadn't, have that damn Modeste Altschuler take care of disposing of his body.

Cynthia reached up and took Sergei's face in her hands. Pulling his head down she kissed him in a way he would remember the rest of his life. She whispered in his ear, "I will be there in the morning and if I were you I would wait for me in bed until I get there. We can order breakfast in your room until 11:30 and I will be there in plenty of time to place the order."

He took one more look at Cynthia, bent down for another kiss and then made his way back to his room. He went directly to his bed and laid down, fully dressed, and slept until he was awakened by someone touching his shoulder.

Breakfast for three arrived promptly at 11:30. Bennie had slept in and when Cynthia knocked on his door at ten-thirty he was dressed but had not made any plans for breakfast. He would join them in Sergei's suite in thirty minutes.

As the three of them sat around the table Cynthia announced that she and Bennie were taking over managing the mechanics of his tour. The schedule was firm, the travel instructions clear, the over night hotel reservations confirmed and all that was necessary was for Rachmaninoff to get to the venue on time and be ready to play his program. Cynthia and Bennie would see that he was.

Last night was described by Sergei as a real pain but that he had managed to make it through the affair and hoped he had not disappointed anyone. There was another he hoped he hadn't disappointed this morning but he didn't speak to that. Benedetto was still a youngster but he could tell that Sergei must have played that part well as Cynthia seemed most content.

Chapter 56
1909-1910

The breakfast was nicely prepared scrambled eggs, bacon and toast. Orange juice to start and excellent coffee to finish with. An American breakfast and it was quickly consumed.

Sergei was trying to sort out his thoughts about what had happened in the last twenty-four hours. He had been standing by the rail ready for disembarking as tired and depressed as he thought he had ever been. The eager faces awaiting him on the dock had sent a sense of foreboding through his soul such that he was tempted to turn away and return to his cabin not coming out until he was back in Bremen.

After leaving Ivanovka he had spent long hours on trains getting first back Dresden and then on to Bremen for his departure on the twentieth of October. Finally getting to his hotel room and ridding himself from the hotel staff, Altschuler and his people and the press he had found himself alone with Cynthia Beckman and the piano tuner. To see her again after almost ten years sent a feeling so good through him that he thought he might be able to live up to what he had agreed to do here in America.

When she sent Bennie to his room and made him lay down for an hours rest he was able to endure the welcoming dinner party. Just barely. He hadn't expected what would happen this morning after she had wakened him.

She had promised him that sometime in the future, when the place and time was right, she would make love to him. She had kept her promise and as he sat at the small table looking at her he thought, for the first time, that he could make it through this tour and still be standing when it ended.

Cynthia returned his gaze and fingered the small locket that was hanging form a gold chain around her neck. He reached over and gently raised it into a clear view and smiled. "I have never taken it off since you saw me put it on in Saint Petersburg. Never. Not even once and I will never take it off," was Cynthia's response to his look.

Bennie wasn't sure what he should do as they were speaking in Russian. He could understand enough of the conversation to tell it was a very emotional moment for them both and that he was not part of it. The knock on the door solved Bennie's problem and Sergei kissed Cynthia quickly before Modeste Altschuler strode into the room.

"Good news and bad news. Everything is confirmed and set up through the sixteenth. The bad news the secretary and interpreter is sick and is not available. I am working on finding another," was Modeste's greeting and almost before he could say anything more Sergei announced that Cynthia would be his secretary, interpreter and manager for them on the road events. Bennie, his piano tuner, would handle all the heavy work and errands. All they needed were the schedules and transportation to the trains and to the venues if they posed problems.

Bennie indicated that today they were to visit the the Steinway Hall and would be picked up in front of the hotel at 2:30 pm and that there was only room for three passengers. Modeste excused himself and told them he hoped they would have a good afternoon and that they would love Steinway Hall. Sergei was excited at the idea of a car ride in the busy New York traffic. He had had a couple of rides in older models on the dirt roads around Inanovka but that was nothing that could compare to what he had just seen here.

As they approached the street in front of the hotel a bright red Buick Model F touring car drove up. The driver jumped out and Sergei took the front passenger seat and Cynthia and Bennie were seated in the comfortable back seats. A honk of the horn and they were off. The driver drove fast, and skillfully, and soon they had made the three mile drive through a busy landscape of roads, horse drawn carriages and a surprising number of cars, none of which could compare to the Buick Model F. Sergei was in heaven as they pulled up in front of 109 E. 14th Street and Steinway Hall.

They were greeted by a guide who was not only handsome but spoke acceptable Russian. As they walked through the main room there were what seemed to be end-less rows of pianos, glistening and waiting to be played. But first it was into the main concert hall that could seat 2000 and on the large stage were two of the Model D Grands, brand new, set in position for two to play. The hall wasn't being used much now as Carnegie Hall had re-placed it as the center of music in New York. It had been the home for the New York Philharmonic for twenty-five years. Sergei and Cynthia went up on the stage and started a tour of the two magnificent pianos. Word had gotten out that someone of importance was there and the hall was quickly filling up. The tall Russian man and the beautiful

American woman were on the stage, with the lighting just right. A sense of some kind of magic was in the air. Sergei sat first and ran through the scales, getting the feel of the keys and then played a number of familiar chords. The sound and tone was fantastic. He nodded to Cynthia and she did likewise at the second piano.

Sergei looked at Cynthia, smiled and nodded his head. She returned the smile and mouthed the words, "Suite number two. I know that one."

It was a delightful six minutes and it didn't stop there as he played the first movement of Concerto Number 2, she following with the second and he finished with the third. Several hundred people had gathered and the applause was well received by them both. They stood, then holding hands walked to the edge of the stage and bowed to their admires.

No one there ever believed for a minute the introduction of Cynthia as Sergei Rachmaninoff's secretary, interpreter and manager. When they were photographed together her look showed it must be much more. There also was no surprise that Rachmaninoff would later insist on only playing Steinway pianos, but that would happen later.

They had a full tour and met most of the staff. It was a nice afternoon and they were driven around Central Park. Sergei was busy asking the driver questions and Cynthia was busy interpreting. It was good that she knew how to drive already so she could give Sergei a better understanding of what the answers meant. If he had had the money at that moment he would have bought the car on the spot.

It had been a fine day and was finished by an enjoyable dinner hosted by Altschuler at his home with the three of them the only guests.

That night Cynthia and Sergei wished Bennie a good evening at his door and went together to Sergei's room where they spent the night together.

Four thousand seven hundred miles to the east was his family, worried and missing him, not knowing what the future would bring. It would be a good future in spite of tragic events that would have nothing to do with this first American Tour. Sergei Rachmaninoff was becoming a star in the world of classical music and the temporary love of another woman would make it possible for him to survive what was about to happen on this grueling tour most would not to have been able to cope with. Certainly not alone.

Chapter 57
2022

Thursday, September 22, 2022 had arrived and so had the premier of Rachmaninoff Concerto Number 5 in the McCallum Theater in Palm Desert. The Desert Symphony Orchestra again to be conducted by Edward Adams with Cynthia Ashbaugh the pianist for this never before heard work.

For more than two weeks Palm Desert was in a heightened state of excitement about the performance of another of the now internationally known, recently found Rachmaninoff treasures, Concertos Numbers 5, 6, and 7. Number 7 had premiered on June 16 and Number 5 was selected for this day with Number 6 to be premiered on Thursday, October 13.

The theater was full, every seat had been taken fifteen minutes before the 8:00 pm starting time. The anticipation was such that it was silent in a surreal way. Everyone was ready. The orchestra had taken their positions at 7:30, positioned their music stands and warmed their instruments. They were all dressed in identical dark charcoal suits and dresses. The material had a light sheen and rich texture, shoes and stockings were likewise uniform. It was the most well dressed and presented group of musicians the patrons had ever seen.

At exactly 8:00 pm Cindy made her entrance with

Ed a few steps behind. An almost silent gasp came from the audience as she made her entrance and confidently walked to the edge of the stage. Her dress was form fitting and of a light, off white material that seemed to sparkle with tiny gray diamonds. Her hair was piled high on her head without a single strand out of place. Her only jewelry was a small, cylinder shaped locket on a gold chain around her neck, The locket sparkled with tiny facets etched into it's gold base. Thin straps held the dress in place and her bare shoulders and arms took on a golden hue. High heels in matching color complemented the ensemble.

Ed made his way to her side and took her hand for the customary bow. His suit was of the same look as was the orchestra members but a shade darker. He was a handsome man, with just a hint of gray at his temples in his otherwise dark brown hair. They made their bows and the applause began in appreciation of a sight one could remember for years to come. Fortunately it had been duly photographed in both still and motion as would be the entire concert.

Cindy took her seat and Ed positioned himself on the podium. With a nod to the orchestra, then a look to Cindy and seeing the tilt of her head, Rachmaninoff Concerto Number 5 was underway.

It was different than any of his other work beginning in a whispering of strings developing into an almost undetectable melody. The sense of melody was established as the piano entered, then was followed by the woodwinds and finally the full orchestra. It rose to a climatic cadenza in the middle of the movement slowing and returning to the beginning melody. Rachmaninoff"s featuring the piano was unchanged and Cindy had done her part.

The second movement moved swiftly into a complimentary composition featuring two more melodies still dominated by the piano. The third movement used the full orchestra to carry the first half and the piano carried on to the finish that resembled the beginning in reverse. The last notes played were from the piano and were later described as a good night kiss on the cheek.

No one knew what to think of this presentation but all knew that for what ever reason they felt a good feeling in their soul. A long needed sense of happiness that all seemed to appreciate. It took a few minutes before the applause started and then it wouldn't stop. They didn't want an encore as they wanted to keep what they now felt and wanted nothing to take that feeling away.

The Desert Symphony Orchestra's members, Ed and Cindy knew this and together applauded the audience. An entirely knew opinion of Sergei Rachmaninoff was in the offing, but you had to have been there in person to understand what it was.

After all the post concert formalities had been taken care of the family made it home and collected together in the music room in Ben and Jennifer's house. Having them here in their house was treasured by them both. All were satisfied. Wilma most of all, saying, "That was the true Rachmaninoff. That what he meant to us, my mother, father and me. He was such a nice man," and her tears came again. Ed was satisfied as he thought their performance had been flawless and Cindy was thinking the same thing. Robert and Sandra just marveled that they could be in such company. Jan and Daniel knew how special it was to be part of this family group and felt they should find some way to be closer to them despite their positions at UCLA and having become part of it's rather narrow society. Allison was intrigued with the calmness that Cindy and Ed displayed after the feat they had just accomplished and the spectacular presence Cindy displayed. BJ had his future determined, and it would be with someone beyond his dreams. At that moment he was just a spectator but in a few hours all of his time would be needed to protect that someone from what was about to happen.

It was John whose mind was elsewhere and wishing that this great game he was a part of was not nearing completion. It had brought more good into his life than all the other things he had done before.

Chapter 58
2022

The family dispersed into the three homes. It had been a wonderful night, all were tired but sleep would not come easily for any of them. In BJ and Cindy's bedroom they had gone to bed, as their norm, sans clothing. He reached to her to caress her shoulders, softly with no other intent. She moved closer and nestled into his arms. "I have never felt more confident than I did tonight. I was so ready and it all played effortlessly. This may sound silly to you but I felt Rachmaninoff's presence. He was there with me. When I did those difficult parts, I could see his smile. BJ, hold me until I fall asleep."

By two in the morning all were sleeping but John who was laying next to Allison on his back. He was satisfied in thinking over the events of the last year. Not even a year as far as arriving at where he was now. So much had happened that had totally changed his life. Love had finally come his way and as he thought this he rolled over on his side to look at Allison as she slept. She lay on her back and the shape of her breasts under her nightgown, rising and falling as she breathed, gave him a pleasure he was now becoming familiar with. Her skin was still good, had a light tan and very few blemishes. His thought then suddenly jumped to Cindy's look tonight and what it was that took him to that place was remembering the small locket she had worn. He had never seen it before. It was different in a mysterious way and he suddenly thought, for some unknown reason, that it was important on it's own. Tomorrow he had some thing to do at the first opportunity. The more he thought about the locket the wider awake he became. He knew he had a special knack of seeing something as small as it having much more importance than just it looks. As the sun rose so did he and he went into Ben's kitchen to find Cindy pouring herself a glass of orange juice,

"Would you like a glass?" she asked as she turned his way and what he saw first was the small locket, which caught a ray of sun shine and sparkled brightly for that instant.

They took the orange juice out to the pool side chairs and sat down. Cindy was used to people staring at her and would just brush it of knowing she was good looking and there was no harm to her if the look wasn't held too long. John's was, but he quickly allayed her discomfort by asking where she had found the locket and told her it had a special look that interested him.

"I was going through the boxes from Wauseon a few days ago and in the one that had the letter box were a number of smaller boxes holding all sorts of collectibles. Nothing important, at least as far I could see. Things that would be in your bathroom or on your dresser. No gold or diamond rings or ruby necklaces. Mostly what looks to be costume jewelry. In one that had some combs and small brushes was a small leather, draw string pouch that had this in it," saying this as she fingered the locket. "Would you like to see it?"

Cindy unclasped the chain and handed it to John. Just then Allison came out with her juice and sat next to

John. As if on cue Julia and Ed showed up and they all got comfortable and began sharing John's interest in Cindy's locket. It was obviously well crafted, beautifully finished and was gold.

Wilma was next and using her walker got close enough to see the locket. "Look at that! I haven't seen one of those in years. I bet you don't know what it is."

She sat down in her usual chair and did her routine to find her comfortable position. Looking up she saw everyone was looking at her for an explanation.

"It is a special locket made to hold a lock of a new babies hair. That looks old and European, or Russian. Where did you find it?"

Chapter 59
1909-1910

The three at the hotel had agreed that their days on the tour would start each morning with breakfast in Sergei's room. Ten o'clock seemed a good time and this morning they had just finished and some plans were being discussed. Sergei wanted a minimum of two hours of practice time alone on the big Steinway. He may want more depending on how things worked out and would like Cynthia to plan on spending an hour with him in the afternoon. Bennie would be welcome to be present but he may find the practicing a bit boring.

As this was being discussed a knock on the door had them meeting Douglas Standish, a handsome and well dressed young man in his mid-thirties. He held a large, plain envelope and explained he was to be their personal guide to the each of the venues on the tour and was employed by Modeste Altschuler.

They cleared the table and he placed the contents on it. Train tickets for tomorrows trip to Northampton, with the time table for departure from Penn Station at 10:30 am. Return tickets were there for a departure from Northampton at 9:00 am returning to the Penn. Hotel reservations for three rooms at the Draper Hotel for the one night and they should be back here by 4:00 pm the next day.

On this trip he would meet them in the lobby at

10:00 am sharp and have transportation to Penn Station waiting at the curb. He would go with them to the station and would be waiting for them on the return the next afternoon.

"Sweeney Concert Hall is the venue and is a beautiful performance space seating 600. It is sold out and a number of extra seating is being arrange for the music students." Douglas said this with an enthusiasm that was contagious.

He placed the train tickets and hotel vouchers back in the the envelope and handed it to Cynthia saying he understood she was managing the tour from their side and he would be working with her on each trip. Most of the planning and reservations had already been done and they would meet before each trip to make sure everything needed was provided. There were several that may pose some special problems and that he would travel with them on any that might present them.

Cynthia's look was not missed by any of the three men sitting close together around the table and when Douglas mentioned his wife was wishing she could make those trips and left it that he might see if she could occasionally be included. He would like them to meet her as she was a music teacher and also a good pianist.

Douglas stood, saying he would see them tomorrow morning in front of the hotel at ten sharp. Wished them good day and took his leave.

Sergei went to the piano and started his practice routine. The first hour was octave by octave exercises, scales, chords and had no entertainment value. Cynthia and Bennie excused themselves and Sergei just asked that Cynthia come back to listen to him play his program for the Smith Concert. It was to be the first completely solo recital he had ever given and he wanted her opinion on what he had chosen to perform.

As Cynthia left Sergei's room his practice continued. She thought that as great a pianist he was he was still concerned about his performance with this so called rehearsal type program. She smiled at this, and was sure she would be helping him with the big time venues that lay ahead.

She was back at two after having taken a walk about the hotel area, looking in windows and going into the park for a short commune with nature in this unusual place.

She knocked on Sergei's door and he answered with a smile on his face. "You have a nice smile Sergei Rachmaninoff. You should show it to others more often but I always want one when we see each other. Even if we have been apart for only a few minutes,"she said and kissing him before he could answer.

"I am playing Sonata number one in D minor, opus 28, Melodie, opus 3, Humoresque opus 10, Barcolle opus 10, Polichinelle opus 3, and Preludes from opus 23, B flat major, F sharp minor, D minor and G minor," Sergei took in a deep breath and added, "Probably the Prelude in C minor for the encore."

`"That is about an hour, maybe a little longer with applause. I have a suggestion. Do you want to hear it?" Cynthia was smiling as she asked this and as she knew he would she continued, "Add about ten minutes from Concerto Number three, start of the first movement. I will come on stage and explain what you will do and about it's premier with the New York Philharmonic on November

28 with Damrosch conducting. It will give everyone something to talk about as they applaud for more."

Sergei looked at Cynthia, who was standing close to him, looking radiantly beautiful. This couldn't be happening but as she kissed him he knew that it was. This tour he had been dreading was going to be a success and he would have Cynthia with him to make it happen.

Chapter 60
1909-1910

The morning of November 3, 1909 in New York City was very pleasant as the three travelers stood together in the lobby of the Netherland Hotel. Douglas Standish meet them at exactly ten o'clock and twenty minutes later, they and their luggage were at Penn Station. A porter had them to their private compartment and settled in with time to spare.

Cynthia thought that was cutting it a little close and decided she would ask Douglas for a little more time on the next trip. It was New York City, but she was from Cleveland, Ohio. She tipped the porter after he had placed their luggage in the overhead rack and he wished them a pleasant journey.

Seats were taken and in a great commotion of bells and steam they were underway. They had five hours of to-getherness and as Sergei and Cynthia had taken the forward seats, Bennie was facing them forward.

Surprisingly it was Sergei who started the conversation by telling Bennie, in Italian, that it was time to get to know his piano tuner. He asked, "Do you know how to tune a piano?" and started to laugh.

Cynthia smiled and looking at Bennie said, also in Italian, "We will be a family for the next three months. On a great vacation adventure and you and I will let Sergei do all the work. Sound good to you, Bennie?"

Cynthia's Dreams

They switched back to English as Sergei wanted the practice to make the questions he would be getting from all directions easier to answer in the manner he intended. Small talk didn't bother him much as it was rarely quoted but dealing with the press was a sore spot. He also knew he was going to have to dodge some questioning on the relationship to one of his constant companions as the tour progressed.

They had a nice lunch in the dining car and were not rushed. The train had made good time and was ten minutes early arriving in Northampton. By three o'clock they had their rooms at the Draper Hotel, a suite for Sergei and small rooms, that did have toilets and washbasins, for Cynthia and Bennie. All on the same floor and not far apart.

It was a nice afternoon so they decided to walk over to the Sweeney Concert Hall. The doors were open and a dozen young ladies, all in white dresses, were milling about excited about the event that evening.

The Hall looked good. Comfortable, had come to Cynthia's mind, as it was the right size for the recital program Sergei planned to perform. On the stage was a gleaming, black grand piano and that is where the three headed. A Mason and Hamlin model that Sergei had played once or twice in the past few years and that he liked. They were made in Haverhill, Massachusetts, just over a hundred miles from Northampton.

Bennie took a quick look and said the obvious, "This is a brand new piano." He pressed the A above middle C firmly and listened. Then three times in a row evening harder. Up the scale an octave and back down two. "Do you want to play it before I go any farther. I think it has just been tuned and it might be better I spend my time talking to a few of these young ladies than messing up the tuning of this big beast."

By this time one of the teachers had shown up, and without introducing herself volunteered that Mason and Hamlin had loaned the piano for tonight's recital. That they had the tuner here yesterday to tune it just right. She was saying this while shaking Sergei's hand, not stopping or letting go until after she had finished.

Sergei told her how much he appreciated having the piano and that he would be sure to tell reporters of having it to play. By this time most of the girls were on the stage and were circling Rachmaninoff in an adoring crowd. Cynthia and Bennie stepped aside and watched the spectacle unfold.

Sergei, a head and a half taller than all around him, bent down and started a conversation asking how many were music students and did any play the piano. Two said yes to the piano question and he invited them to sit on either side of him as he familiarized himself with the Mason and Hamlin.

It brought back for Cynthia the memories of him with the two young musicians as he performed his Trio Elegiaque with them in the apartment in Saint Petersburg ten years ago. That he was so good with young people. So patient and caring that the remembrance brought a few tears to her eyes.

He played a number of chords and notes up and down the scale. Then a group of fast fingerings and he seemed to have touched every key in less than five minutes.

"I am now going to play you a composition that is

not mine but a very special young, American lady wrote and gave to me as a present. She would probably have been a senior here at Smith College at the time she wrote this. This was when she was in Saint Petersburg, Russia in 1899. It was at Christmas time, that year, when I first heard it."

All the young people were now crowded around the piano and Sergei had to asked the two on the bench to give him a little more space. He then played the beautiful piece which only had *1899 Cynthia* as identification.

Chapter 61
1909 -1910

The recital went exceptionally well that night. The Hall filled to overflowing and by some estimate 750 seated and a number more standing, One hundred were seated on chairs in the stage wings, including Cynthia and Bennie.

Following the demanded encore of his Prelude in C-sharp minor came more applause and requests. Cynthia came to the center of the stage and announced, "Sergei thinks you do deserve more and he has a surprise for you tonight, especially for the students. He has just completed his Concerto Number 3 for orchestra and it will be premiered November 28 in New York with the New York Philharmonic, Walter Damrosch conducting. Sergei will play for you his Concerto Number 3 for Piano. It is just over thirty minutes so get comfortable and hold onto your hats!"

Cynthia walked back to her seat with a smile that would have lit up the darkest of rooms. She knew how good this was and soon so would all those in attendance. Some would even say later that what they heard that night had changed their lives.

After all had settled down following the concert, and the three of them were back to the hotel, they said their good nights and went to their rooms. Each were tired but after Cynthia had dressed for bed, pulled down the sheets and tried to get comfortable in bed she laid awake thinking of what her future was going to be. It wouldn't be with Sergei. He must return to his life in Russia, with his wife, his children, and their families. She did not belong there. Her father had told her when she first met him that it was not the right place or time for her to be involved in his life, or his in hers. It was the same now. She knew it must be that way but not for these next few months.

She put on her robe and slippers and went to Sergei's room. The door was not locked and as she entered she saw that he was at the writing desk with a letter in his hand. He stood, placing it back on the desk, and came to her. She would stay until early the next morning. The letter was addressed to Natalia.

This was going to be the routine for them as the tour continued. It was an unbelievably grueling schedule of twenty-six performances, nineteen as pianist and seven as conductor. They were spread out over north eastern America, from Chicago, Illinois to the west, Cincinnati, Ohio to the south, New York City to the east and to Toronto, in Canada, to the north.

The list looked like this with the approximate distance in miles from the home base in New York City added in parenthesis.

Nov 04	Northampton, MA	Soloist	(125m)
Nov 08	Philadelphia, PA	Symphony	(100m)
Nov 10	Baltimore, PA	Symphony	(200m)
Nov 13	New York City, NY	Symphony	(home)
Nov 15	Hartford, CT	Symphony	(125m)
Nov 16	Boston, MA	Soloist	(230m)
Nov 18	Toronto, ON	Symphony	(500m)

Nov 20	New York City, NY	Soloist	(home)
Nov 26	Philadelphia, PA	Cond/Soloit	(100m)
Nov 26	Philadelphia, PA	Cond/Soloist	(100m)
Nov 28	New York City, NY	Symphony	(home)
Nov 30	New York City, NY	Symphony	(home)
Dec 03	Chicago, IL	Cond/Soloist	(820m)
Dec 04	Chicago, IL	Cond/Soloist	(820m)
Dec 09	Pittsburgh, PA	Soloist	(370m)
Dec 17	Boston, MA	Cond/Soloist	(230m)
Dec 18	Boston, MA	Cond/Soloist	(230m)
Dec 26	Chicago, IL	Soloist	(820m)
Jan 03	New York City, NY	Cham/Soloist	(home)
Jan 09	New York City, NY	Cham/Soloist	(home)
Jan 10	Boston, MA	Cham/Soloist	(230m)
Jan 16	New York City, NY	Symphony	(home)
Jan 21	Cincinnati, OH	Symphony	(670m)
Jan 22	Cincinnati, OH	Symphony	(670m)
Jan 27	New York City, NY	Symphony	(home)
Jan 31	Buffalo, NY	Symphony	(400m)

They had three days in New York City before readying and traveling to Philadelphia. He was to play his Concerto Number 2 in C minor, op. 18 with the Boston Symphony Orchestra with Max Fielder conducting. He knew this concerto as well as any of his music and it would be the orchestra that needed the rehearsal. It was one of the best orchestra's in America and the conductor was of the same category. They could get by with a morning rehearsal for the evening performance but that may not be what was planned. He didn't know. The knock on the door would soon give him his answer.

The dishes from breakfast for the three of them

had just been cleared when Douglas Standish made his entrance, holding another large envelope in his hand and a smile on his face.

"I trust you all have seen the schedule for the tour and have a few questions for us. Watching Mr. Altschuler secure the bookings I realized he would leave it for me to do the planning and preparations. First, this winter season is one of the best for the classical music business any of us can remember. Mr. Altschuler is probably the finest agent in New York City and he may have done a bit too much for you on this trip but it is all doable."

Douglas had said this in a calm and charming way that Cynthia appreciated but Sergei was not paying close enough attention to pick up on it. Bennie knew exactly what was happening as he had been around Steinway executives for almost three years doing whatever was needed as he pursued his tuner apprenticeship. What Steinway hadn't discovered yet was what a keen mind he possessed and how intelligent he was. He knew exactly what had happened and waited for Douglas Standish to sell them on the overbooked Rachmaninoff American Tour.

"Mr. Rachmaninoff, Sergei, you are a little over booked and several of the venues are a long ways from here. I think I have made the arrangements such that it will work out and believe me when I tell you your bank account will be much more than you were expecting. Everyone involved will have one of the most profitable years in memory," was said in a sincere and meaningful way.

Sergei looked up and directly into Douglas's eyes. In his best English said, "Tell me how we can get it done!"

Douglas opened the envelope and laid out the contents on the table. "This is for Philadelphia this Monday.

The train tickets are for Sunday morning, returning Tuesday morning, your hotel room bookings are for Sunday and Monday nights. Here is cash enough to cover your out of pocket expenses. The Boston Symphony Orchestra is performing with Fiedler Sunday night and will rehearse with you Monday morning, and afternoon if necessary. They have played Concerto Number 2 several times so are comfortable with a limited rehearsal time. You can do some sight-seeing as the Academy of Music Hall is within walking distance of Independence Square as well as many good restaurants. It should work out fine. Any questions?" was asked and he waited for them to answer but Sergei, Cynthia and Bennie looked at him with signs of concern on their faces, but asked none.

"Well good. I will do everything I can to see you make it through the Tour without problems. That's my job and I am good at it. Baltimore on the tenth is an easy one and the New York Philharmonic knows Number 2 and Fiedler will again be conducting with one rehearsal planned for the morning of the concert. It shouldn't be a problem."

Douglas stood, shook hands with each, received his kiss on the cheek thank you from Cynthia and left the room.

Chapter 62
1909-1910

The tour continued in this way through to the end. There were many highlights and few disappointments. It was exhausting but thanks to Douglas Standish the physical planning went without any major disasters. There were two venues that were memorable, not because of the travel or performance, but in a personal way for Cynthia. The first was the trip to Toronto, Canada.

It was about twenty hours from Penn Station to Toronto's Union Station. Leaving at 9:30 am on November 17 had them in Toronto very early on the concert date of the eighteenth. Sergei was the pianist for his Concerto Number 2 and Fiedler was again the conductor and had left two days earlier to rehearse the orchestra. A morning rehearsal should be adequate for the afternoon and evening performances. Both were full houses of enthusiastic patrons.

On this first morning of travel, after each had settled into their compartments, they assembled into Sergei's to talk over the days activities. Sergei indicated to Cynthia he wanted a few hours alone as he had some letters to write and would like to have them ready to mail as soon as they were back in New York. She and Bennie took the time to walk about the train. It was only about twenty cars and fifteen minutes later they found a table in the dinning car and have a coffee. A bit of small talk and then Cynthia took his hand in hers and asked him for a favor explaining her relationship with Sergei.

"You know that I am having an affair with Sergei. Sleeping with him. Loving him. This goes back to Christmas 1899, almost ten years ago. He was traveling on the same train as I was from Moscow to Saint Petersburg. I was with my mother and father and we, more accurately I, offered him a seat in our first class compartment. I fell in love with him that day and have been in love with him ever since."

She had to stop as all the memories were coming back of that time. The desires she had felt that had not been satisfied then and that she was trying to satisfy now. She couldn't speak of that with Bennie so she went to the point. "I want your promise, your solemn promise, not to tell anyone about this affair. He has a wife, two daughters and a career that has no place for me. Nor should there be. When Sergei boards the ship back home I will stay on the dock and wave a goodbye. I don't expect to ever see him again, certainly never make love to him again. I don't want what I have with him these three months to cause him any harm in the future. There will be suspicions and gossip but you are the only person that knows for certain that we are lovers. I want that to be your secret and to never tell anyone about it."

Bennie sat very still, holding Cynthia's hand and not wanting to let go. "I promise you I will never speak of your personal relationship with Sergei Rachmaninoff. I will tell them of what a special friendship you have with him. It should continue, you know it should, but it probably can't, or shouldn't. Saying goodbye to him is going to a hard thing for you, and for him." Bennie had tears in his eyes as he said this and Cynthia knew the reason. She quickly changed the subject.

"I have a change to our schedule I want to work on and it involves you," was said with relief that she could change the subject. She was still holding his hand and as she felt his grasp on hers relax she released it from his. A smile of a now understood friendship was exchanged and she continued, "I want to spend some time with my mother and father at Christmas. I want Sergei and you to come with me. Just before Christmas we have a break between Boston on December eighteenth and Chicago on the twenty-sixth and we could spend a few days with them then. I will have to see if there is an overnight from Cleveland to Chicago on Christmas day to make it work.

"Another option is in January where we have a five day break before, and another after, our two days in Cincinnati, Ohio. I would like you to meet my parents. Also there is another woman it would be good for both you and Sergei to meet. I think Sergei would enjoy a break like this. I might also teach him how to drive a car," was said with laughter in her voice. "Maybe teach you both!" was added quickly.

Bennie fell more in love with Cynthia but knew it wasn't ever going to be reciprocated in the way he wished. Something he couldn't understand was going on here and he would just let time expose it to him. Before he could say anything Sergei came up to them and sat down in the seat available.

"I have my letters written and ready for mail. Since we have this long trip and shouldn't waste all this time I propose we try some composing together. Not serious composing but as a game. First, Bennie, you don't fool either me or Cynthia. You are a lot more intelligent and smart than you put on, and those traits seldom come in the same package. A piano tuner is fine for now but there is more in your future and I want to watch, and maybe help, you find it. We are going to talk, whistle and sing and when we hear it we will write it. We can look outside and see if there is something that can be described in a song, a poem or in music. If that doesn't do it for Bennie or I we can look at Cynthia and the words will come."

The game of composing was a fun way to pass the time. Sergei had placed several music sheets on the table and gave each a pencil. Bennie was not sure what he could do with it. He was familiar with notes and which key played them but not really the notation. He had an idea but no real skill.

He was first as on the fences that were flashing by were dozens birds and he whistled a bird song he knew which had a unique melody and Sergei quickly penciled in a half dozen notes. Then he whistled them and added a few more. Cynthia sang the notes to Sergei's in a slightly different way and he scribbled in the new melody. "There is a melody to put aside and work on later. Who knows, it may carry an entire movement, or with the right words, a nice song. Next!"

Two hours went by and there were more than a dozen staffs filled with notes. Bennie was a talented whistler and surprisingly could create good melodies. Going through one of the short tunnels he matched the rhythm of the steel wheels on the tracks and the darkness with slow melancholy tune. Again Sergei's pencil jotted the notes on a staff and a few minutes later another melody was placed in the group that held promise.

Chapter 63
1909-1910

The Massey Music Hall was completed in 1894, the interior a neoclassical design featured Moorish arches and was patterned after the Alhambra Palace in Spain. As Sergei entered the space, which at that particular moment was totally empty, he was a bit taken aback. Cynthia and Bennie had chosen to go to the hotel first, check in and locate their rooms. About twenty minutes later they were entering the Hall and had the same reaction that Sergei had except up on the stage he was sitting on the piano bench in front of the big grand piano.

He looked tired, bent forward and had a forlorn look on his face. Cynthia went up behind him and started massaging his shoulders. Bennie had come up and asked if it sounded okay and Sergei replied that he hadn't touched a key yet. He spread his fingers and did his usual exercise and that seemed to help him find his place. He turned to Bennie and asked him to do his thing and he and Cynthia would try to find out if this was the right day.

They didn't get far as the orchestra members were now filing in and in a rather noisy procession finding their seats on the stage. Max Fiedler came rushing down the main isle with a smile on his face, greeted Sergei and accepted the introductions to Cynthia and Bennie.

"We just finished our morning break and are ready for one last run through. You're here so let's see if we can pull this off. The piano is in good tune, according to your stand in, so let's get going!" Max was so full of energy that it helped Sergei enough for a wry smile and he agreed to give it a try. It was four hours until the afternoon performance was to commence.

It went surprisingly well. The orchestra was ready, the conductor confident and once the first note was struck Sergei was at home with the music. He could play it in his sleep and sometimes, like at this moment, had to.

They had two hours left to rest, dress and be back to the hall. The afternoon concert was good and the evening was even better. Most thought excellent. At the post concert party, attended by two hundred special invitees, they were introduced to Hart Massey, a number of his executives and two of his four sons, Walter and Chester. His oldest son, Charles, had died early in life and whose love of music had Hart Massey build the hall in his honor and the youngest, Fred, was out of town on business.

Cynthia and Bennie were standing aside watching the spectacle unfold around poor Sergei Rachmaninoff. He was nearing exhaustion and Cynthia was trying to figure out how to help him. He was looking her way for help when a tall, handsome man in his forties walk up and introduced himself to her. She didn't recognize him at first until he mentioned having lunch with her, and her father and mother, in Saint Petersburg ten years ago.

Her smile and laughter at the remembrance caused the tired Sergei to excuse himself and make his way toward them as having someone looking at Cynthia that way worried him.

The introduction was made and Harold MacDonald was introduced to Sergei. He asked if their small group would like to say their good nights to the remaining crowd and join him at his table in a private club a block away from the hall for a light meal and drinks. It was ten thirty and Sergei, Cynthia and Bennie had only had a hotel sandwich since breakfast that morning.

After they had made their escape and Harold guided them to his club they met an attractive woman and three very pretty young ladies sitting at a private table. Harold introduced his wife and three daughters and a menu of snacks and sweets arrive with appropriate drinks.

Cynthia told the story of her father taking her with him on a business lunch and when she saw Harold approach their table she thought her father was trying to use her as decoy for doing some deal or another. Finding out he was married with children by her father asking about them had taken care of that and she actually found their discussion interesting.

"You know there was more to the story, don't you?" was directed to Cynthia by Harold and all eyes went firsts to Cynthia then back to Harold. "Your father was advising me on the state of the economy there in regards to Massey expanding it's manufacturing into Russia, and other surrounding countries. This was just as 1900 was starting. We were looking to expand internationally. He didn't recommend doing so as he felt the unrest in the peasants, intellectuals and students promoting socialism was gaining strengths and that it was also raising it's ugly head in Europe. I was doubtful about this but Hart Massey had similar concerns and he dropped the idea of expansion and would concentrate on the American and Canadian markets. The 1905 Saint Petersburg riots were the first real indication of him, and your father, being right. Sergei, you might want to consider this in your own plans for the future."

Harold sat back and smiled again. He had a good smile and he was watching Cynthia when he said."Your father told me he wanted to bring you to that lunch meeting to introduce you to the type of man that existed in his world that you might find interesting. Not me, and he was good to tell you I was married and had children, but just to let you know there were ones like me available. I assume something was going on in your life then that he was trying to steer you away from."

The laughter was reserved, and Harold was disappointed in that but the look that Cynthia gave Sergei told him that maybe it hadn't been such a good idea to share the story right then.

Cynthia then smiled, started to laugh in earnest and reached over to pat Harold's arm saying, "That is a story well told and I will tell it again, many times I am sure. In fact, I hope to be home for Christmas and my father will be told it word for word."

Chapter 64
1909-1910

They were on the train the next morning for the return trip to New York City, tired and needing a break. Sergei, especially, was showing signs of exhaustion although he was trying to hide it. Cynthia was trying to help him and Bennie was beginning to think he didn't belong there with them.

At six in the morning they were back to the hotel and at 2:30 pm were to the scheduled recital with Sergei the solo pianist. He would play his regular program of around ninety minutes and add another ten minutes for encores. It was the socializing afterward that really taxed his spirits and Cynthia helped out as best she could.

They had a five day break before the next three programs, but they were together, the twenty-sixth and seventh, in Philadelphia as conductor and solo pianist both days. Unfortunately the twenty-sixth was in the afternoon where as the twenty-seventh was an evening program. An early morning train had them back in time the following the day, the twenty-eighth in New York City as the pianist for the first performance of his Concerto Number 3 in America with Walter Damrosch conducting the New York Philharmonic. Two days later it would be repeated in the same hall.

Three days later he would perform as concerto pianist and conductor on December 3rd and 4th in Chicago.

Three more performances, one in Pittsburgh and two in Boston led to a seven day break that ended with a solo pianist recital back in Chicago, the day after Christmas.

In the early afternoon of December 19, 1909 Sergei and Cynthia lay together on his bed in the Netherland Hotel. He on his back and she on her side with her arm across his chest, both fully clothed and satisfied with just being alive.

Six days until Christmas here in America while in Russia Sergei's wife and two daughters would then be celebrating their Christmas on January 7, 1910 on the Julian calendar. In Cleveland Cynthia's parents had prepared a small tree and would merely exchange a Merry Christmas to each other while missing their only child.

Cynthia was thinking she would like to spend Christmas at home but the idea of adding one more train trip to their schedule had her keep it to herself. Besides, the day after Christmas Sergei had to be in Chicago for, and why it was ever scheduled, a recital.

Sergei could feel her trembling and see the tears on her cheeks. He watched for a few moments thinking what an extraordinary women she was and that he was to lose her in another month. There was no way she could be with him in Russia. Unlike his friend, Fyodor Chaliapin, who managed to have both a wife and a mistress, with children with both of them, he could not do such a thing and certainly never do that to Natalia or Cynthia.

He tried to wipe away her tears and she moved closer to him to be held as she tried to get over her sense of being lost and of losing him. Cynthia knew this was to happen and had been sure could control her emotions but at that moment she seemed to be losing that battle. She also knew that in the last few weeks she had been careless in keeping to her calendar and would soon know whether she had another problem to contend with. She was ready to accept that mistake and he would never be told about it if it had happened.

"Cynthia, I think you should go spend Christmas with your parents. A few days after the Boston concert on the eighteenth you could go to Cleveland and come back here before the January 3 recital and finish out the tour with me then. I can handle the Chicago trip by myself." Sergei said this as calmly as he could as he didn't want to be without her for even one day.

"That is so nice of you to think of that. I want you to spend some time with my mother and father before you go back to Russia." Cynthia had taken a minute to answer and Sergei was worried he had said things wrong but her change in demeanor had him thinking he had said it right. She then continued, "We have some time before and after the Cincinnati concerts on January 21 and 22 and we could spend a few days with them on either side. It would not be hard to schedule as we are here in New York City for four days before and have that much time after them."

It would turn out they would choose to make the visit before going to Cincinnati. Samuel and Rose had already planned to come to Cincinnati and attend the first concert.

Only two more concerts dates would follow and once they were played Sergei Rachmaninoff would board a ship for Russia and Cynthia Beckman would be on a train heading for Cleveland, Ohio.

Chapter 65
1909-1910

Christmas in America had come and gone. Cynthia would spend four days with her parents in Cleveland, enjoy their company and the break from Sergei's American tour. But each night she would lay alone in her bed with tears dampening her pillow. The thought of Sergei going back to his life in Russia, and to his family, was becoming a more serious problem for her than she had anticipated. She had missed her period and was almost certain of its meaning. She would be waiting in Penn Station for him on his return from Chicago and would love him even more but never speak to him about her fears.

Benedetto was with an uncle and aunt, and their extended family, for Christmas and it was his third one without being with his own parents in Italy. It was not going to be that way in the future as he had received a letter from his father that his piano sales business was doing so well he needed him home to help out. As the only son, with three younger sisters, his father wanted him to manage his new location in Venice. Bennie was sure Sergei would understand and he made reservations to be in Italy by the end of January.

Sergei had some time for himself. During the day he spent that time at the piano in his suite at the hotel. He had brought a full box of blank sheet music with him and was sorting through the bits and pieces and putting a few of the melodies in the format of a movement. It had been three months since he had done any serious composing other than a few hours spent on the crossing. It felt good to have the change and time alone to concentrate on composition. At night it was not so good as he had become accustomed to her being near. A needed presence he dare not admit to as to how important it had become for him.

The round trip to Chicago had been brutal but the recital had been well received. He wasn't sure what he was paid but he thought it might be enough to buy a car. At least a small one.

Cynthia and Sergei spent their last month together much more relaxed as the January schedule had only eight performances and half of those were in New York City. They were able to have time outside the rigors of high pressure events and were able to take in the sights of the big city. A highlight for Sergei was his being the pianist for the second playing of his Concerto Number 3 with Gustav Mahler conducting the New York Philharmonic orchestra. It was performed on Sunday afternoon, January 16 in Carnegie Hall. About the rehearsal with Mahler, Sergei wrote:

At that time Mahler was the only conductor whom I considered to be classed with Nikisch. He devoted himself to the concerto until the accompaniment, which is rather complicated, had been practiced to the point of perfection. According to Mahler, every detail of the score was important, an attitude too rare amongst conductors.

Though the rehearsal was scheduled to end at 12:30, we played and played, far beyond this hour, and when Mahler announced that the first movement would be rehearsed again, I expected some protest or scene from the musicians, but I did not notice a single sign of annoyance. The orchestra played the first movement with a keen or perhaps even closer application than the previous time.

The day after what Sergei considered the highlight of the tour he and Cynthia were on the train to Cleveland for a few days with her family. It was a good visit and Sergei's fears of how he would be received by them was misplaced, even when they shared Cynthia's bedroom. Samuel's work as a fund raiser for the Cleveland Symphony projects had brought he and Rose into the social circle of Adella Prentiss Hughes, which was to shape the Beckman's lives for most of their lengthy stay there. She was the prime mover in the establishment of the Cleveland Symphony Orchestra and, eventually, the building of it's home, the Severance Hall.

Adella Prentiss Hughes had almost adopted the Beckmans when they had returned from the three years in Russia and was instrumental in helping Cynthia in finding her way into a position of a requested professional classical pianist. Cynthia had played at Adella's wedding to Felix Hughes in 1904. Samuel's business background found him a natural fundraiser and manager. Rose became the most sought after teacher of literature at the college and her classes were always booked full. Many of her students later credited her as providing them a lifetime of enjoyment by her introducing them to reading.

When Cynthia and Sergei made their short visit his fame was already established in Russia and Europe and was rapidly spreading in America. Adella quickly put together a meet Sergei Rachmaninoff reception on Wednesday, January 19th, with help from the Fortnightly club and he played several of his most popular recital pieces and the two he gave Cynthia credit for composing. He announced them only as *1899 Cynthia*. Sergei promised Adella that he would come back to Cleveland and in the future he did many times.

The American Tour ended in Buffalo, New York on January 31. Three days later Sergei Rachmaninoff boarded the ship that would take him back to Russia, alone but to his home, wife and children. A train took Cynthia back to Cleveland, Ohio to her mother and father's home, alone and six weeks pregnant. Two hearts were breaking and another had just begun to beat.

Chapter 66
2022

October had arrived in Palm Desert. It is a special time of the year as summer has definitely left taking the desert heat with it and the temperatures are perfect. For Cindy and Ed the thirteenth of this month was the key date as it would be that evening the premier of Rachmaninoff Concerto Number 6 would be performed in the Mc-Callum Theater. They had been practicing full time as this piece was different than the rest of Rachmaninoff's other concertos and had a number of unique parts.

The first rehearsal had gone well as all the orchestra members knew how special this was going to be and had been working on their own to prepare. The Thursday night premier and the afternoon and evening Saturday performances had been sold out for months, even before the great performances of Number 5 in September.

Rachmaninoff had this time chosen to be in love with the piano again. It was still his music but the three movements blended together as one piece, six major melodies with hints of others as the movements moved between soft melodies to climatic peaks. The piano was never silent, from the softest touch at the beginning to the full power of the player's capabilities at the end.

As Cindy mastered the piano parts Ed was busy trying to get in his mind on how the orchestra should be conducted. He had reached the point that he could imagine each instrument's contribution and how they should be blended as written in the scoring. A lot hinged on volume as the piano music varied in strength as Cindy was interpreting how it should be played.

"I read that Rachmaninoff and Chaliapin were advising each other on an opera they were performing together, as conductor and singer. Rachmaninoff urged Chaliapin to know the part of every one on the stage. Does that make sense to you?"

Ed took a long look at her. She had borrowed the A Lifetime in Music book from Allison and he had seen her several times sitting alone reading it. A beautiful young woman much more intelligent than one might expect. She had to begun to play a particularly soft melody and as she did he answered, "It does. Knowing what is going on around you is a wise thing to do in life and in music it is no different. That is something I have learned in conducting these last few months. Knowing the sound you should hear from every instrument as the score is written and what it means. As the conductor what you want to hear happening defines your effort. I am just getting to a real understanding of this."

Cindy continued playing and Ed could only marvel at what she could do on the piano. He then realized he had never heard what she was playing and he began smiling. "You composed that, didn't you. I have never heard anything like that before. Have you scored it?"

John came into the music room while Ed and Cindy had been talking and walked up to them just as Ed had asked his question. "The scoring is done and under the bench. I have done several other pieces and I am going to try to compose a concerto for piano using them. Do you like what I just played?" Cindy knew he would because it was a good piece.

John was smiling and started with, "So now we have another Rachmaninoff in our midst. I thought that would be the case but now we know for sure." This halted the discussion about music and Cindy turned toward John saying only, "Tell me!"

John paused before answering. "The DNA results show an eighty percent probability that you are related to Sergei Rachmaninoff. I would like to tell the group when we are all together, if that is alright with you?"

Cindy forced a smile towards John and nodded her okay, then looking at Ed told him she wanted to be with BJ for a while and took her leave.

The week before was when Wilma had recognized the locket for what is was and Cindy had handed it to John to look at more closely. Wilma hadn't waited and blurted out, "It has a screw on top so quit examining the outside and let's see what is inside!"

John had positioned the locket in his fingers and twisted the cap which came off with almost no effort. He then inverted the base and a small paper packet fell into his palm.

By this time BJ had appeared, half asleep with a somewhat familiar smile on his face, and joined in to watch what was going on. Before he could ask any questions Ed and Julia came in from their side and Robert and Sandra showed up from the other direction. It was if the opening of the locket had drawn the whole family together as if by some magical calling. Ben and Jennifer had also come in just in time to watch the happening.

John had opened a clean napkin and laid it out on

one of the poolside tables. He carefully opened the aged paper just enough to see the lock of braided hair it contained. "We don't want to touch this. I think we can assume that this locket was given to Cynthia Beckman by Sergei, or his mother, at Christmas 1899. If it is Rachmaninoff's hair we can have some strands sent to a DNA lab and see if you are related to him. Is that okay with you, Cindy? She nodded her agreement and John made the arrangement with a DNA analysis outfit in Menlo Park, just north of Palo Alto.

John made the announcement the next morning as the entire family had gathered for their usual breakfast together. "It was what we were expecting. Eighty percent certainty, which is very high probability, that Cindy is related to Sergei Rachmaninoff. If it is his hair, which I think we can assume it is, you are his great-great granddaughter."

Cindy looked about her family and they were all taking in what John had just said and smiles and nods came her way which she returned. It was Wilma that motioned her over and she went to her sitting on the side her lounge facing her.

"You knew him as a young man and loved him in your dreams. I knew him in his last years as a young girl and just like he treated you so nice in those dreams he treated me in person. He was such a nice man. It makes no difference if it was the stories your great-grandmother told you of her mother's affair that were what you dreamed, they are your dreams and never, ever let go of them."

Chapter 67
1909-1910

Rose knew immediately what had happened with her daughter as soon as she saw her stepping off the train. Some things cannot be hidden from a mother. Much to Cynthia's relief her father had an important business meeting and could not come to the train station with her mother to meet her. She couldn't hide her tears and beside that she was having her first bout of morning sickness, feeling every bit as bad as she thought she must look.

It was a bitterly cold night and there was several of inches snow covering the ground. Rose had a car waiting and the driver took Cynthia's bags, hustled them into the car and they were home in fifteen minutes. It was warm inside, familiar with the pleasant smell of home. For the first time in three months Cynthia thought she could relax and even knowing what was to come she sensed being where she needed to be.

The tears came again and as mother and daughter stood together, arms around each other, was when Samuel came in the front door excited to greet his only child home. He realized something was wrong and not as it should be for her homecoming. He had an idea what it might be and was certain he and Rose could provide what their daughter would need if that was the case.

It took a few minutes for Cynthia to gain control of her emotions and then she went to her father's for his familiar embrace and kiss on her cheek. He smiled as he fondly looked at her and said in a calm voice, "Welcome home, sweetheart. We have missed you so much and are glad to have you home with us again."

It took a few days to get things settled in the Beckman household but settled they were and Cynthia knew she would be able to handle what was bound to be a tough year for the three of them.

Her mother's position as a teacher at the college was secure as her students ranked her their favorite and her classes were always filled. Samuel's relationship with Adella Prentiss Hughes had grown from a possible fund raiser to a valued advisor and although his income was still based on money he raised it was going to soon be shifted into a salary. Adella had plans underway for bringing back a major orchestra to Cleveland and as that became a reality Samuel Beckman had become one of the men behind the scenes that would help make it happen.

Adella also had another project, the pianist that had helped manage Sergei Rachmaninoff's first American tour. He was now a star and she would need a few stars to help make her plans for Cleveland's cultural awakening happen. The pregnancy bothered her not one bit and she would become Cynthia's best friend, like a second mother and a sister combined.

Rose Anne Beckman was born on September 12, 1910 a healthy, full term baby in the house that she would grow up in, surrounded by a loving mother and grandmother and grandfather. She would mature in the world of classical music, a tall good looking young woman with a nice smile and large, well proportioned hands.

Epilogue
2022

Cynthia Anne Ashbaugh accepted the proof of her being the great-great granddaughter of Sergei Rachmaninoff without so much as a second thought. She was who she was and that the many degrees of separation from him had little, if any, bearing on who she was. It was Rachmaninoff, however, that had formed her life such that it had brought her to where she was at this moment, waiting for Ed's nod for her entrance as pianist playing the recently discovered Rachmaninoff Concerto Number 6.

It would be deemed the finest concerto those in attendance had ever heard and the recording would match the performance. The Saturday afternoon and evening performances were of equal quality. No one present had been disappointed and all were thrilled to have been there.

The Sunday morning following Saturday's concerts found the Palm Desert family having breakfast together conversing about what many others, now worldwide, were just learning about. The classical music press were beside themselves with what had just been presented to them.

John and Wilma were most satisfied, he as his last effort with the back in time technology had been such a success in both execution and resultant value. For Wilma it was her living her last years being it's witness. Ed and Julia were satisfied with what life had provided them and how well their children were doing so far in theirs. Smiles had crossed their faces as BJ and Cindy had come out to the pool area barefoot, dressed as usual in shorts and T-shirts, and looking like the young lover's they were. Their talents were unfolding before them and would provide their parents the happiness one derives from watching their children's accomplishments.

Robert and Sandra had planned time on their sailboat as they finished their fictional book, The Life and Times of Sergei Rachmaninoff. It was in the hands of the publishers and any more efforts on their part could be accomplished on-line. They were planning on a slow sail south, through the Panama Canal, a springtime run up the U.S. East Coast and an early summer crossing of the Atlantic Ocean to Europe.

Ben was slowing down but with Jennifer making his last years so good he refused to acknowledge his own aging. He had no complaints, and he marveled at the life his beloved granddaughter, Julia, was living as he watched her move about among this remarkable group that had formed around him.

Allison looked over her new family and could only smile at what it had brought to her. Just a year ago she feared she was becoming just another Santa Barbara widow, plowing through the rest of her life looking for the unattainable and now she was part the most exciting group imaginable. She had even taken an impossible trip back in time, with Ed and Cindy, to visit Sergei Rachmaninoff.

BJ and Cindy were in love. He had discovered something he could do that had little to do with the math and science he had been studying, the management of a newly discovered classical pianist. It would take a talent that came naturally for him along with the discipline of the physical sciences that aided in his decision making. As the demands for Cindy as a pianist and concert soloist increased she welcomed the challenge and appreciated BJ's calm management of her time. She had the confidence that was so necessary to play at that level and it was thought, by those who knew, it might have been something to do with her genes.

At Ed's suggestion the third bedroom in their house was turned into an office for BJ and Cindy to use as the demands on her time began to mount. A large desk and chair was in place, as were two filing cabinets and a table. Two comfortable chairs faced the desk and the small closet was set up to store all that needed storing. There was a nice bookcase into which the Proxmire book collection had been placed. Cynthia Beckman's grandmother's books would be properly displayed.

Cindy was sorting through the banker boxes to decide what should be kept in the office, placed in their room, about the house or stored in the garage. BJ had gone out for a while and she was enjoying the quiet and privacy. Five of the seven boxes held things of her parents that she decided could spend time in the garage. She sorted through them quickly but as she started to close up the last of the five she noticed a music book had slipped out from under some household papers. As she lifted it out she could see more music books and loose music sheets.

As she worked down through the stack the memories came back of all the time she had spent at the piano with this music. Her mother and grandmothers had spent much of that time with her and had helped in developing her skills. One book, titled Rachmaninoff Piano Solo Edition, Second Piano Concerto had caught her eye. A 1946 copyright of forty-six pages. It was what was slipped into the center fold that startled her most. A nine by twelve folder contained six old, folded and slightly smaller music sheets covered in penciled notations, bar after bar, staffs filled with erasures and corrections on almost every sheet.

Reading the first four bars told her what it was she was holding. "My grandmothers knew. My mother knew. They all knew but never told me about Cynthia Beckman and Sergei Rachmaninoff," saying this out loud as she sat on the floor surrounded by her music books and sheets, holding onto a past that had determined her future.

Back In Time

At another time and a different place Sergei Rachmaninoff, and all those around him, were to have much to live through. Their time and place on this earth had the ground under their feet trembling. Following his American tour his financial success had been insured but not so for his own future or happiness.

As he watched Cynthia Beckman standing on the dock, off to the side of the large American crowd that was bidding him farewell, he could not see the tears streaming down her cheeks. He saw her wave and he had waved back, sadly thinking that he may never see her again. He would, and many times, but it would be first almost ten years later in a different place and under much different circumstances.

Rachmaninoff had returned to Moscow as an international celebrity in demand for performance as pianist, conductor and composer of new works. He found the three not compatible and chose the performance and conducting the route to wealth. Most of his later compositions had been hidden away to be discovered long after his death.

As World War I waned the Russian Revolution commenced and by the early 1918s the Rachmaninoff family had been stripped by the communists of most of their property, including his beloved estate, Ivanovka. An opportunity for a Scandinavia tour would allow for Sergei, his wife Natalia and their two daughters, Irina and Tatiana, to escape Russia. His sister-in-law, Sophia Satina, would join them and she would spend the rest of his life as part of the family. His last concert performed in Moscow was held on March 25, 1917. They lived in a collective apartment in Moscow until they were able to take the train to Saint Petersburg, then leaving from there on December 22, 1917 for Finland with visas for the Scandinavia tour. A very difficult winter passage by train and horse drawn sled around the Gulf of Bothnia to Denmark found them securing shelter in the home of a friend's house in Copenhagen, exhausted, broke and having only a few cases holding their remaining belongings. He played ten recitals on this tour which providing some, but insufficient, income.

On November 1, 1918 the family boarded the SS Bergensfjord in Oslo, Norway. Eleven days later they arrived in New York City. It was a wartime crossing with no exterior lights showing and interior ones curtained. The Bergensfjord was approached twice by British warships but was identified and allowed passage. Donations from friends and admirers funded most of his expenses. He and the family checked into the Hotel Netherland, the second time for him and the first for his family, in America still impoverished and in debt.

He started on a full time seasonal tour routine that had him eventually performing concerts over most of the United States, Canada, Great Britain and Europe, He did this year after year, including the start of 1943 when he became terminally ill and died on March 28th. At that time he was one of the highest paid entertainers in the world.

Leokadiya Kashperova's life would also take a number of turns for the worse during this time. She was a year older than Rachmaninoff, had graduated twice from the Saint Petersburg Conservatory and established herself as a coming star, both as a pianist and composer. In 1916 she became a music teacher at the Smolny Institute, met Sergei Andropov, a young student, and married him that same year. Unfortunately he was a Bolshevik leader with ties to Lenin. As the Smolny Institute was being used as the headquarters of the revolutionaries in Saint Petersburg, they were forced to flee to Andorpov's parents home in the Rosto-on-Don to avoid his arrest.

In 1920 Leokadiya moved to Moscow, which had settled into a more normal post revolutionary life, but her public appearances were few and her compositions ignored. It would be the recent discovery of some of her compositions by Dr. Graham Griffiths, while he was researching a project on Igor Stravinsky, that has bought her into the public realm again.

As result of Adella Prentiss Hughes's efforts to rejuvenate the Cleveland Symphony Orchestra it would become one of the premier orchestras in America. Nikolai Sokoloff, a Russian violinist and conductor, was asked by Adella to visit Cleveland to appraise another one of her projects, a music school for children. He stayed fifteen years and was instrumental in Cleveland's cultural revival. He and Samuel Beckman formed a management team, with Samuel working behind the scenes, that helped in making Cleveland the classical music and cultural center Adella Prentiss Hughes so badly wanted. On February 5, 1931 The Cleveland Orchestra, the name changed, hosted a gala concert at the newly completed Severance Hall located in the city's University Circle area. Another of Hughes's projects had been completed and she garnered the name, The Mother Of The Cleveland Orchestra. Two years later she would retire.

Sergei Rachmaninoff made his first appearance in in Cleveland, since his visit to the Beckmans in 1910, to perform a recital on November 17, 1919. It was then that he met the nine year old girl that he thought he had known before. Her mother he knew and he would see them both many times over the next two decades. He would book twenty-one recitals and concerts in Cleveland until his last appearance in 1942. During these years his faithful wife, Natalia, would travel with him keeping him company and the loneliness away. They would spend time with the Beckmans when opportunities arose. His booked appearance for Cleveland in1943 had to be canceled.

On June 12, 1934 Rose Anne Beckman married George Albert Whyte. They made their home in Appleton, Wisconsin. Three generations later, Shirley Catherine Mason Ashbaugh gave birth to Cynthia Anne Ashbaugh in the small town of Wauseon, Ohio, less than six hundred miles from where it had started but more than five thousand miles from where her story actually began.

ABOUT THE AUTHOR

Art Myers was born in 1935 and grew up in the small southern California town of La Mesa. He graduated from San Diego State College in 1958 with a BS Degree in Engineering. Several employments in the Military Industrial Complex lasted until the end of 1969. His first layoff was in 1961 and he spent the fall months working as construction labor in Mammoth Lakes, CA and the winter of 1962 skiing in Aspen, Colorado. Another stint in engineering and a second layoff occurred which found him with a wife, daughter, house payments and just beginning what became a thirty year career as a professional sculptor. Interspersed in that thirty years were a variety of residences and occupations for both he and his wife. Retiring in 2002 they bought a sail boat and spent ten years living aboard and cruising both US Coasts. They have lived in a variety of places including Saratoga, CA, Aspen and Loveland, CO, Lake Forest, IL and currently Vero Beach, FL.

His first book was an autobiography, *My Story, How A Young Boy From California Ended Up An Old Man In Florida*, written for family and friends in 2015. He has now completed six works of fiction, *Andrew's Piano, Ed Adams Chases A Dream, A New Life For Robert Johnson, 10,000 Years Before Present, Ed Adams Touches The Stars* and *Cynthia's Dreams*.

www.ingramcontent.com/pod-product-compliance
Lightning Source LLC
Chambersburg PA
CBHW071431200726

48294CB00002B/589